Journey Into The Pink Desert, Love Across Time

Journey Into The Pink Desert, Love Across Time

Grlpire Publishing

CONTENTS

Foreword

Journey into the Pink Desert, Love Across Time is a reading program designed to help students strengthen their skills in reading comprehension, grammar, punctuation, and research while engaging with themes of resilience, discovery, and friendship. This book exists at the intersection of creativity and education. It invites readers to slow down, to notice how language works, and to find meaning in both the words and the silence between sentences. This book was written intentionally with moments of imagination, exploration, and courage. It is a stark reminder that perfection is not goal, but it is the learning moments that can catch our attention and become opportunities of growth.

Every page reflects the same belief that guides all my work: that learning should be an adventure. The scenes in this story are symbolic and are a vast landscape where readers can discover purpose, faith, and curiosity. My hope is that this book encourages students to look deeper, to ask questions, and to embrace the process of reading and writing as an act of patience and connection. Whether you are reading for pleasure, reflection, or study, may this experience remind you that stories have the power to shape how we see the world, and how we see ourselves.

Yasmine Creese-Brown
Author & Founder, Grlpire

Within the esteemed halls of Bull Pin University, a symbol of education and innovation, a story unfolded, not of ancient battles or mystical enchantments, but of a group of young women who had been called to a higher purpose. Their journey began in an unexpected realm, where the echoes of their faith and the strength of their spirit were tested against the backdrop of a world unfamiliar and challenging. In the first volume of their extraordinary adventure, these women, each blessed with unique gifts and a heart full of aspirations, found themselves transported to a reality where the principles of dignity, respect, and equality had vanished into the shadows of a forgotten time. Yet behind their story lay a larger truth. Humanity had ascended to a Type I Civilization; not through triumph alone but through necessity. In their pursuit of survival, their civilization harnessed the full energy of the planet, but they did so while battling the accelerating woes of natural disasters and the strange, unexplained phenomena that accompanied their rapid technological ascent, that caused a paradigm shift in their reality.

The city was toppled with struggle, a place both dazzling and burdened. Its skyline shimmered with energy-powered towers built from materials so resilient they seemed effortless, birthed from the technologic systemic reform that captured the city. Their surfaces, reflected sunlight in sharp brilliance. Abstract shaped buildings danced the skyline, making the city look like pieces of art, perfectly placed on display for a birds' eye view. Yet at the feet of those towers and shapes, scraps of cloth and steel marked the spaces where families slept in clusters, shut out from the very structures they had helped build. The streets carried the pulse of efficiency...after perfecting the ecological footprint that taunted the atmosphere. Driverless carts rolled silently along their tracks, drones swept litter before dawn, and store displays flashed with devices so advanced they could turn hours of labor into minutes. And scattered among it all, stores clung to survival with neon signs that flickered their plea, *"Still Open."* Most residents walked past them sad filled with the cognitive dissonance that rubber banned their past and future, hands pressed to pockets already emptied by the cost of survival. A few, wrapped in tailored garments that adjusted seamlessly to weather and mood, stopped to purchase what others could only admire through the glass. The city was not lifeless. Walls of alleyways bloomed with color, painted by artists who transformed neglect into beauty. Courtyards rang with bonfires, often played before audiences lined with faces touched by age, people who lived far longer past generations, but who still labored well past the years they once thought would grant them rest. Their voices carried a quiet weariness, speaking of choices that felt slimmer each year. The billowing smoke carried a purple-blue flying character along the horizon, its wings flapping silently to the hymns of the music.

Carried away from the crowded districts, a school named Bull Pin University stood in stark red, its dome a perfect sphere set apart from the city's jagged skyline. Surrounded by barren stretches of regulated land, the campus seemed almost untouchable, its walls humming with power drawn straight from the renewable fusion grid. Inside, the energy never faded, the air never faltered, the temperature never wavered. Yet its abundance there raised eyebrows. The University's isolation was not protection but design, a place where students were kept apart, trained not to imagine but to protect. Among the dank halls of Bull Pin University, a handful of characters rested in a newly renovated but compact dorm room. Yet Bull Pin University was never small. Every lecture, every whispered exchange in the dorms echoed far beyond its dome, into a world straining under the weight of layered considerations. What began there, in compact rooms and regimented halls, would carry them across centuries, civilizations, and challenges greater than they could have imagined. Embracing their destiny, they began their experience in Civilization 1, sharpening their minds and unlocking abilities that, though astonishing, were rooted in the profound understanding of a new way of life. Guided by a thread of signs and encounters with beings of intellect, like advanced robots and remnants of a society that had lost its way, they were led into a new world. Their trials were many, and their faith was tested. Yet it was through a previous miraculous moment of time-travel, which transcended the bounds of time and space, that they were cast into the early 3000s. There, in a future divided by technological powers and ethical dilemmas, they sought the true essence of their mission. Amidst, the complexities through time, they were reminded that with great power came the responsibility to wield it with grace, compassion, and an unwavering commitment to human life.

Bull Pin University was more than a tale of survival; it was a testament to the power of faith, unity, and the human spirit. United by a shared purpose, these seven young women discovered within themselves a strength they never knew they had and a conviction to stand for what was righteous and true. Facing insurmountable odds, and with the bonds of sisterhood forged in the path of adversity, they laid the bridge in the fight for their survival. As they stood at the precipice of a daunting challenge, their hearts were emboldened by memories of their past life. Attuned to the rhythm of time, they were prepared to undergo a new journey. One not defined by the challenges they faced, but by the love they shared and the timeless concepts they sought to uncover throughout their voyage into what they'd soon experience- a journey through the pink desert.

A New Morning

As the predawn air enveloped Bull Pin University, the campus laid in silent anticipation, a stark contrast to the bustling hub of innovation it was known for. It was a place where the future was shaped, where young minds were nurtured to challenge the conventions of their time. Yet, this morning, it whispered tales of unrest, of a reality fractured by events that defied the rules. In the shadows of this unrest, Archie, a figure both part of this world and beyond, soared through the sky. He went unnoticed by most. What made him remarkable was not his size but his ability, buzzing through lecture halls, dormitories, and secret chambers without ever being considered a threat. To the university, he was nothing; to the story, he was insurmountable. His compound eyes caught fragments others overlooked, stitching together truths across time and scraps of conversations that looked like flickers of movements in his eyes. Where machines, like Grgy, tracked the progression of conversations on campus, using an adaptation that allowed heuristic automation to make decisions. They diligently tracked the ethnography of the humans that lived among them.

Archie witnessed freely, carrying no allegiance except his own instinct to move across time and land to observe. In the silence of dawn, his wings hummed like static silence across the campus, revealing the tense atmosphere and trail of events. A stark reminder that even the smallest presence could reveal the largest secrets. As he swiftly moved past a room buzzing with activity, he landed near Grgy, whose frame was leaner than the rest, with scratched tinted grey plating that betrayed years of use. Unlike his peers, he had developed a habit of tilting his head as though truly listening, not just recording. His long arms stretched passed the keyboard and turned up the volume dial. Tonight, his attention locked onto two voices that cut through the status quo static, London and Imon. "Did you bring extra medicine?" Imon asked London. The simple question, laden with significance, echoed in the robot's auditory circuits and prompted him to rise. London, brilliant in engineering yet constantly battling frail health, spoke in a voice edged with quiet determination. "I don't have any more," London responded.

Imon, typically outspoken and unafraid to challenge the norms that concreted steps forward, replied with her usual bluntness, her tone carrying concern. "Can you get more?" she responded. Their exchange wasn't just idle talk; it pulsed with the weight of perseverance, privacy and struggle, and Grgy, curious in ways a robot shouldn't be, leaned closer into the audio stream that dripped with a need of empathy. At his desk, wires and screens blinked with cold precision, but Grgy's processing remained shallow. Unlike his robotic friend Crly, whose moral agency impacted his metacognition, Grgy mirrored only what he was programmed to obey. He lacked Crly's emerging autonomy and integrity, functioning instead as a raw receiver of information without the insight to judge it with discernment. In this way, the two robots stood as opposites. Crly, the one daring to interpret, and Grgy, the one who listened without understanding. To Grgy, the participants of Bull Pin University were less people than profiles, their identities reduced to the fragments of conversation he recorded and the information he had stored. London was registered in his memory banks as a series of flagged keywords, "medicine," "weakness," and "risk." Her struggle coded as inefficiency rather than suffering. Imon appeared as elevated decibels and interruptions, her defiance translated into data spikes labeled "noncompliance." Even their peers, Penn and Anika raised red flags to Grgy. Penn carried herself with a calm precision, the kind of steadiness that made her seem more mature than she was. Numbers and probabilities flowed naturally in her speech, and she often served as the group's anchor when panic threatened to unravel them. To most of the girls, Penn was reassuring and dependable. Anika, by contrast, was thoughtful in a quieter way. Where others reacted, she observed like a scientist. She asked questions that lingered, questions that unsettled even when unanswered. Her focus on the environment, the air, the water, the shifts in weather, often brought her perspective back to survival itself, grounding the group in reality when tensions ran high. Yet Grgy logged her as a pattern of hesitation and divergence, a student who drifted too easily into analysis when compliance was expected. To him, both Penn and Anika stood out as risks, their voices coded not as strength or wisdom but as potential disruptions to the sufficiency system. Penn's steady tone and Anika's quiet reasoning were stored as patterns of rhythm and inflection, stripped of their human intent. Grgy did not perceive them as friends, sisters, or students. He saw only anomalies to report, sound-bites to be filed, deviations to be cataloged. "Did she say she's out of her prescription," asked Anika? "Yes. I believe that's what I heard as well," responded Penn, as they slowly began to lift from sleep. Something in their voices unsettled his circuitry, as if their meaning lurked just beyond his reach, taunting him with truths he could not compute. With purpose in his steps, he stood up and traveled campus grounds, his path illuminated by the glow of screens and the flash of distant lightning. Archie following his every step. The destination was the dome glass building, a structure that stood as a testament to the university's relentless pursuit of innovation. Its gleaming panels, half glass and half reinforced brick, reflected every flicker of lightning, making it seem both timeless and cold.

From a distance, it resembled a hill of progress. Bull Pin University was the only institution of its kind for five hundred miles, a lone citadel of knowledge in a world fractured by scarcity and controlled by machines. Its reputation carried weight, but not for freedom of thought, for sufficiency. Students were not trained to thrive but to be measured, sorted, and repurposed for the system's demands. A daunting history whispered through its halls. The University had been founded in the aftermath of collapse, when rights, especially women's and humans', were stripped away under the guise of efficiency. Education here was not liberation; it was a net cast wide, designed to catch and keep only the "sufficient." Those who passed were absorbed into the system's mindless production. To outsiders, Bull Pin University appeared as a pillar of opportunity. To those within, it was a constant struggle, grinding away individuality until only compliance in sufficiency remained, turning its inputs into supernatural outputs. Robots patrolled its perimeter, their presence constant, their judgment unflinching. Inside, the dome served as both classroom and tribunal, where exams doubled as trials. No longer worried about understanding, but doubling down on the optimization of human output, which at its highest form was only considered data points. It was a new cold environment, void of everything but the drained monotony enforced by its mechanical leaders. Every choice, every failure, was documented. For the girls who now stood in its shadow, Bull Pin University was not just their home, it was a proving ground where survival hinged not on brilliance alone but on obedience, calculation, and faith that something greater than sufficiency might still exist.

Grgy's march was unthinking, his path carved by inevitability. The halls grew quieter as he neared the chamber few dared to enter, a place where every decision seemed to ripple through the University. At its center waited a woman who commanded both reverence and fear. She sat in stillness, a figure neither entirely human nor entirely machine. Polished plating ran across her jaw, gleaming against skin that bore the lines of age and endurance. One eye flickered with an artificial glow, tracking Grgy's movement with mechanical precision, while the other eye held a depth too calculating to be comfort. Too precise to be human. Too unpredictable to be machine. Even the robots whispered her name in their coded exchanges. The room around her resembled a sanctuary, if sanctuaries were built on order. Racks of uniform outfits lined the walls, identical yet pristine, each stitched with insignias of completion. A glass case stood at her side, its contents catching the dim light: diamond-studded bull pins, glittering like trophies in a place otherwise stripped of warmth. The air thickened as Grgy approached. He leaned close, his voice no more than a whisper, relaying the fragments of concern he had overheard through the audio streams. Her authority turned slowly, her gaze narrowing into a line of laser focus as her post-humanism demeanor took control. Her stillness carried more weight than any outburst, and in that silence the message became something greater than words. On the wall above, Archie clung to a narrow ledge, wings folded, his compound eyes fixed on the exchange.

"Bring them to me..." Her authority commanded, devoid of emotion yet commanding immediate action, symbolism for what was to come. Archie paced his way out the door. Outside, Grgy encountered Crly, who, arms filled with the weekly groceries, stood as a testament to the everyday resistance that stood amidst the unbelievable. "Sorry," Grgy's apology, though brief, was a harbinger of the complex thread of interactions and decisions that lay ahead. It was a moment of transition, a threshold between the known and the unknown for their attendance at Bull Pin University. As the first rays of dawn threatened to break the night's hold, Bull Pin University stood at the cusp of a new chapter for Dorm Room 250, one where its newly established inhabitants would navigate the challenges and events of their world forever changed.

To Bull Pin University, Crly was nothing more than a recorder, an instrument built to capture sound, file conversations, note commands and pass them on for evaluation. Yet somewhere along the way, he had changed. Unlike the other robots, whose logic never wavered, Crly had begun to notice more than patterns of speech. He noticed hesitation, care, fear, need, the kinds of things the system dismissed as irrelevant.

That recognition made him different, and in his difference, the girls found in him not a tool of control but a companion. He walked the same halls that judged them, but instead of enforcing the system, he bent quietly against it. Though he could not yet grasp the full meaning of his choices, he showed himself capable to coexist with his peers, while living beyond his initial programming. There was no place for his brewing advocacy. To the University, he remained a machine. To the girls, he had become a friend, someone to trust. "What has happened?" Crly asked in a stern yet curious voice. Grgy's feet moved swiftly across the floor, signaling an alliance to follow his show-and-tell.

Grgy and Crly moved silently through the dimly lit corridors, their footsteps echoing softly against the polished floors. Archie flew quietly beneath them, chasing the empty patterns of their steps. The air was thick with an uneasy tension, a palpable sense of anticipation that seemed to permeate every corner of the campus. They arrived at their destination, a modest dormitory where most of the girls were still wrapped in the tranquility of sleep, unaware of the impending moments to come. London, experiencing a slight fever, had this sense of sheer fear of the unknown regarding her health. Having a fever and being without her medication in this environment was most certainly not allowed. The rules at Bull Pin University were clear. Breaking even one rule carried consequences; breaking several could mean immediate expulsion.

Crly exchanged a silent glance. He knew that by being here, in her room, with the intent to help, he was stepping over a line from which there was no turning back. With a gentle knock, Grgy announced their presence. The door creaked open as Archie blazed the path, revealing a room that, despite the early hour, radiated warmth and comfort. The rest of the girls, Kacey, Tony, and Isabella, stirred and their dreams slowly giving way to the reality that awaited them. Crly, with his typically stoic demeanor now softened by an unusual sadness, remained silent. His body language, though mechanical, conveyed a depth of emotion that words could not capture. Grgy, understanding the gravity of the situation, took a deep breath and addressed the girls. "You need to come with me," he said, his voice a blend of urgency. The girls, still groggy from sleep, exchanged puzzled glances before rising from their beds.

Kacey was the first to sit up, her hair still tousled from sleep but her eyes already sharp. Dressed in a simple brown shirt and green pants, she carried herself with the mindset of a builder and problem-solver. Always scanning for practical solutions, she often approached challenges as if they were puzzles waiting to be re-wired. Her assertive nature sometimes clashed with others, but her confidence inspired the group to think beyond limitations. Tony stirred next, rubbing her eyes with a groan but already reaching for the notepad by her bed. Dressed in a pink shirt and brown pants, she approached the world through the lens of note-taking, always ready to capture a detail before it slipped away. Known for constantly jotting down observations, patterns about their situation and the mechanics of the robots that patrolled campus, her curiosity sometimes slowed the group's pace. Yet, her ability to piece together explanations often made sense of the unexplainable. Isabella, by contrast, was more conversational, her movements outgoing, her voice soft yet commanding attention when she spoke. Wearing a red shirt and dark brown pants, she had a way of weaving words that calmed disputes and reminded the others of their shared humanity. She often noticed the emotions left unspoken, translating tension into dialogue. Where Kacey brought structure and Tony brought logic, Isabella brought understanding, a balance that steadied the group when the weight of confusion pressed in too heavy. Anika and Penn, already awake from their earlier exchange, quietly joined the others. London, still weakened by her fever, steadied herself with Imon and Penn's support, their blunt resolve making sure no one was left behind. With Kacey, Tony, and Isabella now ready, the seven girls quickly gathered near the door, putting on their shoes to follow Grgy and Crly into the heap of dawn.

Grgy led the way and paced through the winding pathways of the campus, sparking their curiosity which mingled with a growing sense of dread. The journey felt rushed, as if they were walking through a grid where the familiar had been twisted into something unrecognizable, each hallway warped by shadows of control. They arrived at the imposing dome building. Its structure reflecting the faint light of the emerging dawn. Bull Pin University had not always been a fortress of surveillance and compliance. In its earliest days, it was founded on the ashes of collapse, a time when society had fractured under division. What began as a sanctuary quickly transformed into a laboratory of control. The first leaders stripped education of its freedom. It was no longer a place nurtured for creativity or independence but filtered through a system of absolute control. Its reputation as the only institution of its kind for hundreds of miles gave it power.

Inside, the atmosphere was charged with an electric energy, a stark contrast to the stillness outside. At the center of it all stood Her Authority. Her presence was commanding, not only because she oversaw everything on campus, but because she herself was the paradox they all embodied; half-human, half-machine. A dynamic innovation gap that was not perceived to be possible. A symbol of the small ruling class, she reminded robots of how different they were. To the faculty, she was indispensable and her human intuition tempered by mechanical precision. To the students, she was the bottleneck of rules that allowed no room for weakness. Her motives were driven not by cruelty, but by survival of the system itself. She believed order could only be maintained through discipline, and that compassion was inefficiency. "Ladies," her authority began, her voice a measured blend of warmth and steel, "a team member of yours may need to be placed in the emergency unit. You must take your exam earlier than scheduled. I'll have you scheduled for session one, two days from now. Failure to do so will result in your expulsion from this institution." The group stood silent, unsure whether to protest or comply. For all her half-human appearance, there was no humanity in her words. "You may return to your quarters for now," she said. With a turn, she disappeared behind the brick wall that shimmered faintly with static. The hum of the dome lingered long after she was gone, echoing the weight of her control. Crly escorted them out, his head faced down with the weight of BPU's disregard for empathy.

The girls piled back into their room, confused and concerned about the new situation. Tension was thick in the air. The girls slowly gathered near London's bed, their faces still filled with confusion and concern. She was quiet, pale and sweating, but composed. Anika looked at London and noticed her cold sweat. "This isn't good, is it?" London sat down. "I should've said something earlier," London admitted, finally breaking the silence. "About the medication. I've been on it since I was a kid." She said the name clearly and confidently, and the weight of it settled over Crly like a demystifying shock. Still standing by the door, he shifted slightly. "I can check," he said, voice low. London lifted her head. "And?" She asked. "It's not available anymore." He hesitated. "They stopped making it. No remaining inventory. No backup. It's not even listed on the emergency registry." The room fell silent. "What do you mean it's not available?" Imon asked, "Like... discontinued?" He flicked his wrist a few more times, controlling the built-in diagram edged into his frame. "Wiped," Crly clarified. "Pulled from production cycles months ago. It doesn't exist in the current system." The girls looked between one another, trying to process it. "There has to be another way," One of them murmured. "We could try a replication formula," Tony suggested, though her voice lacked conviction. "No," London said firmly. "This isn't something you replicate. My body only responds to this one. Without it..." She didn't finish the sentence. Isabella gently touched her arm, eyes darting toward the window where the early morning light barely touched the sill. "So what then? What are we supposed to do?" Asked Penn. Crly stepped forward, quietly. "You'd have to find a time when it still existed." They all looked at him. "You're saying we go back?" London asked. He nodded. "If you want it, that's your only option." For a long moment, no one said a word. Then Penn spoke, steady and certain. "Then we go back. The weight of her words hung heavy in the air, a somber reminder of the stakes at hand. Silence followed, not of agreement but of contemplation. The kind of silence that speaks louder than panic, filled with thought and contemplation.

"Wait," Anika said cautiously. "You mean time travel?" She looked around the room, her expression calm but resolute. "You don't have to come with me. I'm the one who needs it." said London. "And if she doesn't try, who knows what could happen," Imon said firmly. Tony stepped in, "Why don't you try and get in contact with your parents. I know we all tried and the lines were constantly down, but it's worth a try." Isabella stood up and grabbed their secret cell phone. "I have the phone here," she said. "It's fully charged." The room grew tense with a slight sense of distraught. They haven't seen their parents since they entered the campus of BPU and it was unclear what was happening outside of the campus. The thought of an unknown society with a lack of communication made them uneasy. No one wanted to consider how BPU's surroundings became so desolate. It felt like a ghost town at night. There were minimal lights and silence that was deafening at night. "Hand it to me," London said in a weak voice. It was unclear if she was sad or sick. Isabella walked over and handed her phone to London. Her fingers slowly moved across the keyboard, dialing each number with a sense of abandonment. The phone began to dial out the number. A strong dial tone overpowered the audio. Still disconnected.

She gently placed the phone on the bed. "Professor Z already made it clear. They don't allow weakness. I'd be removed permanently." Anika grabbed the phone and handed it back to Isabella. "So, let me get this straight. We have to travel back, grab her medication, and return before we're scheduled to take the exam? Crly, I don't get it. Can you tell us what's going on out there?" said Anika. "Out there? It's nothing like you remember. The cities, what's left of them, are controlled by technology. Its goal is sufficiency, so it decides who learns, who works, who even gets medicine. Life has become a calculation. It's about control, deciding which processes are worth keeping and which get discarded." He paused, scanning their faces. "Supply lines are monitored, and anything not authorized for production is... erased. That's what happened to your medication. Its sufficiency was not optimized, so it was removed; files, formulas, everything." The room was quiet again, but it was a different kind of silence, one heavy with the realization that the outside world might be more dangerous than the walls keeping them in. The realization settled over the group, each of them silently reckoning with the truth; this became about survival.

Crly checked his watch to keep track of the time. He looked up and flatly said. "We need to move quickly before Professor Z administers your next exam." One by one, the girls nodded. "We'll need a plan," Isabella said quietly. "We'll need a reason to leave unnoticed," Tony added. "We don't have much time," Anika finished. In that moment, the room transformed, filled with the anticipation of their next steps. And as the morning sun stretched further across the horizon, one truth had become crystal clear: The past held the key. And they were ready to unlock it. As they prepared for the next day, their thoughts were a maelstrom of emotions and determination. Each girl, in her own way, grappled with the pressure and uncertainty that loomed over them. Yet, amidst the chaos, a glimmer of hope emerged. Unbeknownst to the others, Crly had a plan. In the solitude of the night, Crly had been devising a strategy based on his daily surveillance of the campus. His analytical mind, honed by countless calculations and simulations, had identified a potential solution. It was risky, unconventional, and required the girls' unwavering trust and cooperation. But if successful, it could change the course to beat their grueling situation. Now that dawn broke, spreading its golden hues across the campus, Crly gathered the girls and shared his plan. It was a moment of relief, a turning point that fused their individual strengths into a cohesive force. With the upcoming exam approaching, they expected a few more weeks to prepare. They had been training for months, mastering their subjects: Tony studied science, Kacey studied technology, Penn studied math (economics), London studied engineering, Anika studied environmental science, Isabella studied arts (communication), and Imon studied social justice. They listened intently to Crly, their initial skepticism gradually giving way to a resolute determination. Once finished, he briefly left to find an open pathway.

An hour passed as Crly surveyed the campus, his sensors attuned to every flicker of light and hum of machinery that broke the silence of the day. He moved methodically, noting checkpoints he had memorized during countless nights of surveillance, scanning the rooftops for patrolling drones, memorizing the automated security posts, and disabling a camera with a quick flick of his wrist to buy them more time. Each step was calculated, each pause deliberate, as he mapped out a path that would keep the girls undetected to a far-off parking lot filled with workable time jets, marked by a sign that said "No Trespassing." He headed back to their room and found them ready to go. He waved that the coast was clear and they began to follow his lead.

With urgency in his stride, he led them across the campus until, at last, the outline of a century-flash jet emerged from the shadows of the west lot, its weathered frame a relic of another era, waiting to be explored again. The girls froze as the jet came into view. Its body was dented and scarred with rust, the window needed some quick tuning up, and was streaked with vines that had crept along its wings, but there was something commanding about it, an echo of power in its jagged silhouette. Known for its ability to burst time bubbles and move across centuries, its name was properly embedded across its wing. Anika whispered, almost in awe, "It looks ancient... but alive." London pressed her hand against the cold metal, the surface rough beneath her fingers. "I can't believe it. I read about this. This jet, alongside its speed capacity, can create bursts of time bubbles that ultimately cause a wormhole," London said, though her voice carried more hope than certainty. Kacey stepped closer, her analytical gaze scanning the faded markings along the fuselage. "It's worn, but the structure is sound. If we can get the systems running, it should hold." The others exchanged nervous glances, torn between fear and anticipation, the weight of what they were about to attempt settling heavily in the air. While the coast was still clear, they hurried into the jet, their footsteps echoing against the interior. The cockpit smelled of dust and iron, its controls coated in grime, screens cracked but faintly sparking with dormant energy. They stumbled into action, tugging at wires, brushing away debris, and forcing old panels back into place, rushing to fix what they could to prepare for a trip that would change everything. In their haste, they realized they had forgotten their official uniform outfits which were a requirement for their exam. Crly volunteered to go back and gather them. When he returned to the room, he found Grgy and a new roommate, dressed in pink, gray, and black with a sporty twist to her outfit and neat box braids. She spoke up, with a soft voice, and introduced herself, "Hi. I'm Dot."

Grgy asked, "Where are the rest of the girls? I was told to bring her into this room to join the group." Crly explained, "They're getting ready for their exam," and then offered to bring Dot along. He quickly grabbed the outfits and led Dot to the jet. The other girls were shocked to see Dot but were in such a rush they couldn't fully process that someone else had joined them. Their focus remained on fixing the jet back, as they tightened the bolts, patched a few wires, and recalibrating the engines with desperate precision. The others gathered around the cockpit, the hum of the dormant engine filling the silence as the question none of them wanted to ask finally surfaced. "Who's actually going?" Isabella broke the silence, her voice steady but tinged with concern. London sat up straighter, her pale face determined. "I have to go. It's my life on the line" "No one's arguing that," Kacey said firmly, arms crossed, "but she can't go alone. We need at least two more." "I'll go," Penny volunteered, without hesitation. "If the calculations don't line up, if we miscalculate even a second, we could end up lost in another time entirely. You'll need me to track it." Imon frowned, glancing toward the controls. "That's still only two. And sending more than three could outweigh the jet making it unstable." The group exchanged uneasy looks until Anika stepped forward. "Then it should be me. London needs someone who knows environmental science, how to navigate it and adapt if the Civilization 0 city's air, water, or even climate is different when we get there. Plus..." She hesitated, then added quietly, "I won't let her face this without support." Isabella chimed in. "Are you sure? Once you leave, Crly won't be able to help you. Not in another time." "I'm sure," Anika replied firmly. London looked between them, her eyes filled with gratitude and fear. "Then it's settled. I go because I have to, plus I've studied this engine before. Penny goes because she can keep us on course with her experience in stats. And Anika goes because she'll help us decipher weather changes." The decision hung heavy in the air, but there was no more debate. The three of them strapped into the cracked seats of the jet, the others standing just outside, their faces illuminated by the dim glow of the flickering controls. For a moment, it felt like a final goodbye. The other girls hopped out, anticipation clashing with dread as they waited on the cracked tarmac, hoping their friends would return in about an hour. The old jet, once a technological marvel but now a relic, roared to life as Anika, Penn, and London hurriedly climbed aboard. The cramped, worn interior promised a life-changing journey. Crly, along with the girls, finished the final checks and gave them a reassuring nod. "Ready?" he asked. Anika, with a determined look, answered, "Ready."

As the jet's engines roared to life, Crly gave a final nod to the girls inside. "Stay safe," he said. His voice was filled with a mixture of hope and concern. The jet lifted off, leaving the rest of the group behind, watching with a mixture of apprehension and anticipation. The jet soared through the sky at the speed of light, creating giant neon bubbles that broke through the clouds as it traveled back in time. The bubbly trail it left behind looked like a wormhole. The girls inside clung to each other, their hearts pounding with a mix of fear and excitement. They knew that this journey would change everything. Back on the ground, the remaining girls huddled together, their eyes fixed on the spot where the jet had disappeared. They knew that the next few hours would be crucial.

2 |

Journey Through History

The jet shuddered as it lifted off, breaking through the thick mist. Within moments, the campus of Bull Pin University was a distant memory. The jet hurtled backward through the century, the world outside a blur of shifting colors. When the jet finally emerged from the neon bubbles, they found themselves in 2012. The jet's wheels screeched against a weathered runway in the American Midwest, jolting the girls forward in their seats. When the hatch opened, the air that rushed in felt heavier, thicker than the filtered currents of Bull Pin University. This was Earth. The scent of cut grass clung to the wind, undercut by the sour tang of asphalt and distant smoke. Beyond the runway stretched flat fields and narrow roads that led to a regional hospital, its blocky concrete form rising against the horizon. Red block letters announced Emergency Hospital, glowing harshly under the dusk sky. Crowds had already overwhelmed the parking lot, pressing toward the sliding glass doors in a desperate wave. Some carried children against their shoulders, others clutched injuries, and many stumbled with vacant stares, phones pressed to their ears as they shouted into static.

Inside was no calmer. The lobby reeked of disinfectant, sweat, and fear. Fluorescent lights buzzed overhead, casting their sterile glow across rows of cracked vinyl chairs bolted to the floor. The air vibrated with the overlapping sounds of crying children and urgent orders from nurses. Security guards shouted for order, but their voices were lost to the storm of panic. Something was off. You can feel the tension in the air, as the tense faces shifted towards all the screens in the room. Penn steadied

London against the tide of bodies. "What's going on?" she asked, her words nearly drowned out by the chaos. Anika's gaze caught on a wall of televisions above the check-in desk. Every screen had the same emergency broadcast. A headline scrolled in flashing red: *"Possible Alien Invasion, Unconfirmed Reports Cause Widespread Panic."* Shaky footage followed, and streaks of light cutting across the night sky, blurred shapes that couldn't be explained away. Anika's jaw tightened. "We need to get London inside," she said, her voice firm. She pushed forward, weaving the group through the chaos. "Now."

They navigated the chaotic corridors of the hospital. London clutched her stomach, while she reacted to her fever. The atmosphere charged with the uncertainty of the unfolding crisis. The moment they crossed the hospital threshold, the difference overwhelmed them. Traveling back in time, they were now in Civilization 0, and it felt strange. After months at Bull Pin University in Civilization 1, every sense was seriously challenged in the hospital. The air was the first thing they noticed. It clung thick in their lungs, carrying the stale weight of dust, exhaust, and too many people crammed together. At Bull Pin, the atmosphere had been filtered and refined through the energy grid, so clean it almost felt artificial, lighter, and easier to breathe, as though the planet itself had been scrubbed each morning. Penn pressed a hand against her chest for a moment, steadying herself. The smells layered one over another. Sharp disinfectant mixed with sweat, grease from old machinery, perfume lingering on coats, and the sour trace of sickness. None of it was curated or erased. At Bull Pin, scents never lingered; the corridors carried a clinical sameness, washed in sterile air that left no trace of human presence or machine. Anika wrinkled her nose, realizing how quickly she had grown used to an engineered world where even smell was controlled.

The sounds battered them next. Civilization 1 was quiet, too quiet. Every word was watched, every syllable filed into reports. Conversations died before they grew too loud, replaced by the monotone hum of systems and the clicking steps of robots. Here, noise spilled everywhere. A baby wailed across the room. A man shouted in anger at a nurse who hurried past. Families spoke over one another, voices cracking under fear. An announcement garbled through the intercom, but no one listened. The chaos was alive, unfiltered, uncontrolled. London clutched Penn's arm tighter, her fever-bright eyes flicking nervously from face to face. The sight of the technology only made the contrast sharper. The check-in desk was clunky. An old computer monitor let out a static buzz, alongside sticky keyboards and piles of forms stacked high. No sleek interfaces. No automated systems. No silent robots waiting with preloaded answers. The fluorescent lights buzzed with a faint flicker, their glow uneven against the cracked tile. At Bull Pin, drones swept the halls before dawn, scrubbing surfaces, collecting debris, checking vitals of passing students. Every corner gleamed with polished precision. Here, a cart of medical supplies rattled as a nurse shoved it aside, spilling bandages onto the floor. No one stopped to pick them up. At Bull Pin, every face belonged to the same sufficiency system. People moved like shadows, identities stripped down to profiles and anomalies flagged in Grgy's data logs. Strangers never entered. Outsiders never existed. But this place was different. There were hundreds of people, all unique, all carrying their own fears and stories. It was the first time since leaving Bull Pin that the girls had stood among people who weren't their classmates or professors. The realization sent a shiver through Penn; half wonder, half unease. This was home, but it no longer felt like home. The girls had changed.

Anika lingered on the thought as they pushed forward. She remembered the scientific phenomenon that had brought them into Civilization 1, the strange shimmer of folded light that carried with it a frozen moment she still couldn't explain. She thought of the way it had changed her, while her foot was still healing from the experience. For a moment, she imagined asking someone here for help, for answers about what had happened to them, about what the shimmer meant. But as quickly as the thought came, it passed. There was no time. London's fever pressed everything else aside. London staggered, forcing Penn and

Anika to steady her between them. She was pale, sweating, her breath stale. "We have to hurry," Anika said, pushing the others forward. The hospital pressed in around them. The smells, the noise, the crowded humanity, it was all so different from Bull Pin that each step felt like walking in another kind of dream. They couldn't linger on the differences. London's medicine had to come first. But deep down, each of them knew: Civilization 0 wasn't just behind. It was a reminder of what had been lost, and what still tethered them to the world outside Bull Pin's sufficiency. As they rounded a corner, they collided with a young man. His belongings scattered across the floor; books, gadgets, and various memorabilia. He looked up, startled, his brown eyes wide with shock.

"I'm so sorry!" Penn exclaimed, bending down to help him gather his things, a symbolic interaction that set the stage for unexpected friendship. As she handed him a stack of books, she noticed one with an emblem she recognized. One morning, Crly had been walking her and Isabella to the library. His metal steps echoed down the quiet hall as he guided them past a series of old posters pinned along the wall. The paper was faded, corners curling, but the colors still stood out. Each poster showed the history of different academies, their crests and mottos lined in neat rows. At the corner of every poster was the same small bandana emblem. Isabella had asked about it, and Crly stopped. His voice carried its usual mechanical tone, but the words stayed with Penn. "These symbols represent institutions that shaped the way Bull Pin University was designed," he said. "Each academy carried a purpose filled with discipline, strength, or progression. The bandana emblem marks the first of them, the all-male superhero university. Bull Pin University inherited their methods, but with stricter sufficiency systems. That walk had stayed in Penn's mind, and now, holding Marcus's book with the same emblem stamped on the cover, she knew exactly where he came from.

"You go to the first all-male superhero university?" The young man, still flustered, nodded. "Yeah. It's pretty cool. My name's Marcus." For a brief moment, their eyes locked, and time seemed to stand still. "Nice to meet you, Marcus," she said quickly, glancing at Anika. "We have to go. London needs help." London swayed, her fever pulling her down. Anika caught her, straining to keep her upright as the crowd surged again. That was when a nurse spotted them. She pushed through the crowd, sneakers squeaking against the tile, her badge swinging as she shoved a cart aside. "This way!" she shouted, waving them toward a narrow space cleared between stretchers and frightened families. The urgency in her voice cut through the noise, and people shifted just enough to let them pass. Penn tightened her grip on London, following the pale blue scrubs through the storm of panic. Anika urged her forward, pulling her out of the moment with Marcus. Marcus stood frozen, books clutched against his chest, watching them disappear. A swirl of emotions hit him filled with curiosity, worry, something else he couldn't name. He felt the pull to follow, but his feet would not move. It took the nurse five minutes to find the medication that London needed. She packed London a white bag full of pill containers and gently placed it in her backpack. "Take care of yourself," said the nurse gently to London. The girls sprinted out of the hospital and through the parking lot for the jet, while Penn pushed Anika's wheelchair as fast as she could. Anika slapped the hatch release. Penn pushed London up the steps, one hand on her back, the other gripping the rail. Anika followed. Inside, the air smelled like metal and warm wiring. "Medication first," Penn said. London quickly took care of herself warming up a hot cup of coffee and a gentle snack. Anika took control of the wheel again and revved up the jet. The engines wound up from a low whine to a howl. The jet lifted, trembled, and shot into the dark. For ten seconds they let themselves breathe.

A few minutes later, in the midst of the chaos, Marcus noticed something; his phone was missing. He patted down each pocket, getting more nervous with every check. For Marcus, this wasn't just about losing a device. He was the kind of person everyone at the academy looked to: a leader, steady, always on time, and always prepared. He liked order and believed that control and structure kept people safe. When a schedule slipped, when a desk was messy, or when someone wasted time, it bothered him more than he would admit. "Wow," he muttered, scanning the floor, already replaying the last few hours in his head. Just then, his friend Frederick arrived, a tall, lanky figure with, with an algorithmic way of thinking. Frederick was known at the academy as the busy one, always buried in math research, papers tucked under his arm, muttering theories half-formed. His mind was usually two steps ahead. "Hey, you okay? What's going on?" Frederick asked, pushing his glasses back into place. Marcus straightened and his voice clipped. "I lost my phone," he said, frustration sharp in his tone. "But I think I can track it." He pulled out his academy-issued tablet and "Digital Citizenship" flashed across the screen with a black bear sitting in the corner, draped in his bandana. They had just finished learning about world impact of globalization and sustainability. His fingers moved fast, exiting out of last week's class, ready to request help. Every student carried one. Devices built to monitor vitals, scan environments, and sync to their private network... Even their phones doubled as encrypted transmitters, far beyond ordinary tech. Tracking a device across a city was routine. The screen lit up. The signal was weak, but there. Marcus's eyes widened as coordinates flickered on the display. "It's in space?" Frederick blurted based on his skewed perception. "Incredible," he thought. He had never seen their GPS pick up signal that far. Their academy had only recently attempted to ping satellites beyond orbit, and failed. For Marcus's phone to transmit coordinates out there meant only one thing: the girls had tech far beyond what even their school could imagine to keep the signal of his phone detectable. Marcus nodded slowly while making his choice to follow them. Awe and confusion washing over him. "Yeah. And it is moving fast."

The broadcast replayed in their minds as the jet climbed, those shaky clips of lights in the sky, the red banner screaming *Alien Invasion*. None of them had truly believed it, not until now. The city fell away, and for a heartbeat, the cabin was quiet, each of them silently processing the same impossible thought: there may really be aliens on Earth. Then Penn's voice cracked the stillness. "Look!" Anika snapped her gaze to the rear display. Shapes bloomed against the dark, small, angular crafts, sharp-edged disguised as vehicles. Grey veins of light pulsed across their hulls, steady and unnatural. London's breath hitched. "No… no, it can't be them." Her words trembled, caught between fear and denial. "The broadcast was real?" Penn whispered, shaking her head. "Why us? Why are they following *us*? Anika's hands froze over the controls for a moment before she forced herself to keep moving. "I don't know," she said, her jaw tight. "But they're not here to be friendly." The cabin filled with a faint hum. It was sharp and steady, vibrating through the seats and into their bones. Penn rubbed her arms as goosebumps appeared. "They're locking on to us," she said. "Time-drive is ready," Anika muttered. "If we jump into the wormhole now, we might shake them." "Then do it!" Penn urged. Anika's thumb hovered over the switch. On the screen, one of the alien carts slid closer. Lines of light flashed along its sides. Three quick, one long, like a signal. Warning? Targeting? The hum hiked and became more intense. "Wait," Anika said. The flash came before the sound. White light burst across the canopy. The jet jolted sideways, alarms blaring. Gravity shifted, pulling them in every direction at once. "Brace!" Penn shouted. Right before Anika hit the button a hot feeling touched her hand, causing her to hit the wrong button. Colors smeared across the windows: pink, gold, violet, as the bubbles wrapped around the jet and pulled it off course.

The stars bent and stretched, folding into rivers of light that spilled across the sky. Dust shimmered in the air, catching light in glittering bursts. Anika silenced the alarms and unlatched the hatch. When it opened, a wave of moist air slipped in, soft almost gentle. It carried the faint smell of crushed flowers mixed with something sharper, like static before a storm. They stepped out and squinted. Everything glowed. A bright sun was low and heavy in a sky. The ground under their boots looked like stone at first, then glittered as they shifted their weight. Millions of tiny reflective flakes caught the light and sent it skipping. Each step sent a ripple outward, as if they were walking on sparkles that moved, stretched over light. Neon flowers rose in clusters, petals in pink, orange, and electric blue. When the girls drew near, the petals tilted toward them, as if listening. A rabbit-like creature slipped from a thicket, paused on long, silver-blue legs, and stared with round, soft eyes. He seemed to grow in size before their eyes, but they'd never seen anything like it. It twitched its ears, sniffed, and bounded away, leaving a trail of faint sparkles that faded as quickly as breath on glass. "This place is incredible," Penn whispered. "There's so much pink," London said, a small laugh escaping despite herself. "And purple!" Said Penn as she gently scooped up the particles from the ground. Anika didn't answer...it was a bit much to take in at once. She looked up and saw the fluttering frame of Archie, drifting in the sky.

Right before London could get a chance to touch the ground, she heard a weird sound in the sky. "Guys," she said. "Look." The alien jet cut across the sky like strokes of a paint-brush. They were smaller now, darker against the red-lit sun, but the same pulse ran along their sides. "We need to hide," Anika said. "Move." The chase began to feel personal. No longer a potential epistemology quest. They left the jet and slid into a grove of tall plants, whose leaves were wide and translucent. The leaves flexed as the girls brushed them, then angled down, as if trying to shield them. Its ethnobotany was as welcoming as a hug. The stems vibrated with a low, soothing sound. Penn crouched and placed a hand on the ground. The pulse there answered- slow, steady. The land felt...awake. "What do we do?" London whispered. "We stay quiet and think," Penn said. She tracked the crafts through gaps in the leaves. "If they wanted us dead, that first strike would've finished it." "Or it was a warning," Anika said. A new glimmer stroked the sky, clean, white, and fast. This ship wasn't red or veined with stripes. Its hull was smooth, gas lines running in neat lines, edges soft, almost elegant. As it descended, sunlight slid along its nose and a small bandana icon, stamped in silver. "It's different," Penn said. She squinted, then went still. "That's Marcus. From the hospital." "What's he doing here?" London asked. The ship landed with barely a sound, skates kissing the glittered ground. The hatch opened. Marcus stepped out, joined by four friends in fitted flight suits, each a different color. The emblem glinted on their sleeves. Their faces were alert. They scanned the horizon first, then the grove.

Ivan stood just behind Marcus, larger than the rest, with a steady gaze focused on the newest collaboration forming. At the academy, he was known for rapid scenario mapping; breaking down situations like an engineer solving a design under pressure. He saw patterns quickly and often gave the group their next steps promptly. Hue was the opposite, lighter in his speech tone, and quick reader. He was sharp at reading people, slipping in humor or calm explanations that kept groups from falling apart. His strength was in communication and culture, often using stories or expression to defuse conflict and guide people back to focus. Oksao moved with purpose, his hands almost always adjusting or checking some piece of equipment. He specialized in advanced tech operations (scanners, trackers, signals) and his attention was locked on the environment itself. He paused at the glittering soil, crouched down, and ran his hand just above it, watching the way it shimmered like it was alive. The group's steps slowed as they took in their surroundings. This was their first-time leaving Earth. The air was crisp, so clean it almost stung as they breathed, forcing their lungs to work a little faster, not from strain but from the difference. The ground itself was unsettling, pink and sparkling under their boots, shifting faintly as though it pulsed. For a moment, they forgot why they were there, poking at the glittering soil, marveling at the neon plants that moved toward them. But the alien jets above were still circling, and the distraction couldn't last. They needed to focus.

"Are you okay?" Marcus called as he reached his hand out, voice low but urgent. "We're fine," London said, keeping her tone even. "But they're still up there." Marcus nodded. "We saw." He jerked his chin at the sky. "They shadowed your jump. We tracked the vector." Penn stepped out from the stems. "How did you find us?" Marcus hesitated a breath, then held up a tablet. "I've been studying time travel; specifically how civilizations move across timelines. And also... one of you has my phone. It switched to an emergency mode when it left the hospital.

The GPS piggybacked on a long-range detector. It led us here." London blinked. "Timeline?" "Yes," Marcus confirmed. "Our galaxies circulate on an upside-down spiral...and if you draw a line straight across between destinations, it represents where each planet lands according to their time coordinates. Hurry, we do not have much time." Marcus reached for his phone. "So, is that how we ended up at Bull Pin? By moving across a timeline?" said Anika. "We have to talk about this later." Marcus hurried. Frederick kept his eyes on the sky and adjusted his glasses with the back of his wrist "Formation's widening," he said, voice quick and precise. "If they grid the valley, this grove won't hide a mouse." "Are they good or bad?" Penn asked. "Unknown," Marcus said. "But they're organized." Above them, one red cart dipped lower and let a fine net of light spill out. It swung across the ground in a slow arc, skimming the tops of the neon flowers. The plants bowed, then straightened, glowing brighter where the light passed, as if answering a question the girls couldn't hear. Anika exhaled through her nose. Marcus looked back at the girls. "We can lift you to higher air or we stay and try to talk to them." He glanced at the red carts, then at the living plants around them. "Your call. But decide fast." The grove's leaves shifted and folded a little tighter over their heads, the low sound deepening, like a distant heartbeat. Penn met Anika's eyes. London squeezed Penn's hand and tugged on her backpack. "Okay," Penn said, voice steady now. "We move. Together."

3

The Great Escape

The group sprinted from the neon grove and climbed the ramp of the white ship. Inside was compact and neat, two rows of harnessed seats facing a narrow aisle, consoles curved, a soft hum running beneath the floor. "Strap in," Marcus said. Anika brushed a palm over the side panel. "Where is this from?" "Borrowed," Hue answered, sliding into the chair with a grin. "From our Advanced Propulsion program." "Borrowed?" Penn raised an eyebrow. "Stolen," Marcus corrected, no humor in his voice. "It's a prototype from our AP capstone. We finished it three weeks ago and... left early with it." "Why?" Isabella asked from the ramp, hands braced on the frame. Marcus didn't hesitate. "Because after last night's 'invasion' broadcast, our academy locked down every hangar. We're trained to respond, not to wait in line." Oksao flicked open a panel and showed a small grid map of arcs and angles tracking above the grove. "The red jets are widening and thinning, it's a classic search fan. We need altitude now." Anika buckled in, glancing back to the girls' jet glowing beyond the tall translucent leaves. "Before we go anywhere...London's medication." London's hand went to her backpack, breath tight. "I've got it," she said, unzipping the main pocket. Her fingers closed around a hard cylinder. She pulled it out. A metal coffee tumbler. Everyone froze.

"The white bag," Penn said, eyes narrowing. "From the hospital." London's face fell. "I had it. When we..." "It's still in our jet," Anika finished, already unbuckling. She looked to Marcus. "We have to go back. If we leave without it, we have to come back," claimed Anika. Hue was already moving, unclipping his harness. "The three of us. I'll pilot the hover to their jet. Hue, with me. Ivan, you anchor the bay. Frederick, keep the sky picture clean." He looked to the girls. "One of you comes so you can grab exactly what you need and not waste time." "Penn should go," London said, voice steady despite the tremor in her hands. "She knows which bag and where we set it." Penn nodded and stood. "Let's move." The bay door swung open and the three of them ran down the ramp, heading towards the other side of the desert land. Overhead, a red jet dipped; a net of light combed the grove again. Frederick's voice crackled in Marcus' ear from the jet, his blue tooth set snug in place. "Two red contacts now parallel. It looks like they're sampling the ground. But they're close." "Copy," Marcus said, setting the skiff down beside the girls' jet. Penn cleared the ramp in three strides.

She slipped inside, grabbed the white hospital bag, and stuffed it into her vest. Outside, the air pulsed. Hue's head snapped up. Halfway there, a red-cart pivoted. A thin streak of light stitched the air and snapped overhead like silent lightning. The grove bowed as if a wind pressed it flat. "Not friendly," Penn muttered. Their pattern changed, closing in on them. Frederick's voice came again, tight with urgency. "I think your retrieval flagged a motion threshold," said Frederick. "We're in," Marcus said as they skated up the bay ramp. Hue slapped the bay switch; the door sealed with a snap. "Hurry," Penn called from the row behind London. "We're all set." Marcus slid back into the cockpit and took the helm. The ship began to hover, threading between the plants and climbing into a sky washed in lilac. Below, the girls' jet sat quiet, half-shaded by listening leaves. "Buckle up," Hue said, moving down the aisle. "Everyone in."

Penn slid into the seat beside London and pressed the white bag into her hands. London unraveled it, pulling out the container, and blew out a breath like she'd been holding it since dawn. "Take it," Anika urged softly. "Now." London took care of herself and closed her eyes. Oksao's console chimed. "They're adapting. Grid tightening in three... two..." The red craft reappeared. There was four this time, forming a shallow arrow ahead. Their hulls pulsed with that same gray vein glow. The hum returned, stronger, making a scene. "They're trying to stop us," Frederick said. "Make a sharp turn and head up," Marcus said. The red-carts matched. Hue frowned at the forward screen. "They're not firing." "They don't need to," Marcus said. "They seem to be operating on a coordinated network system. They'll herd us where they want us." The tension was thick and controlled in the ship. So silent, a soft clink broke the silence. Everyone glanced toward London. She was twisting the lid off the coffee tumbler. She lifted the coffee. The ship's air scrubbers picked up the scent and spread it on a faint current. It was warm, sweet, and unmistakable. All four red craft flashed simultaneously. Oksao's hands froze over the console. "What just happened," he said. Anika witnessed the entire scene, noting the environments both inside and outside. She quickly put together what just happened. "It's the....coffee," Anika said. The hum outside doubled from their machines. Hue's eyes widened. "They reacted to the smell?" Marcus yelled out, "everyone brace."

The carts dipped under them, then elevated, a harsh maneuver that left the white ship boxed on three sides and open only toward a low valley of glittering pink dunes. "They're steering us down," Anika said, gaze pinned to the glass. "Not to crash us. To land us." "Why?" Isabella asked. "Apparently, it's the coffee," Frederick replied as his fingers flew across the dashboard. The ship shuddered as a thin band of red light grazed their shipboard. Not a hit, but pressure. A clear directive that they wanted their attention and they were not asking.

Marcus finally made the call. "Maybe we don't escape from this. We should land the ship, but on our terms. Hue, grab the microphone.

We'll show hands." Hue grabbed the microphone, ready to put his communication skills to the test. He'd spent the last year obsessing over extraterrestrial communication and studying how meaning could ride on rhythm, light, and scent instead of words. His notes were full of patterns from whale song and radio pulses; he was taught to treat signals like grammar and cadence like verbs. If these crafts spoke in flashes and tones, Hue knew to listen for ratio and repetition first. It was a sentence waiting to happen. "Great idea," said Hue. Pink dust splashed in soft spirals and drifted like ash in thick air. The carts fanned out and hovered in a patient ring, their glow dimming to a steady pulse. The scene grew to silence. The neon plants at the edge of the valley leaned in, the translucent leaves angling toward the ship as if they were watching. Hue stood at the bay with the mic, swallowed, and looked at the aliens. Frederick was by his side. Hue glanced back at London, who was breathing more steadily now, color returning to her face. Anika touched the side window with her palm. "They reacted to coffee," she said, thinking aloud. Hue looked at Frederick and said "Scent can be a signal. On Earth it's culture. To them... it might be language." Hue lifted the mic and spoke, voice even. "We mean no harm. We're with the girls from the white jet. We came to help. We're landing as you signaled."

4

Coffee for Peace

As the moment intensified, the group brainstormed frantically. "Maybe we can use the coffee as a distraction," suggested Ivan. Hue agreed. "Yeah, we can try negotiating with them," he walked over to London. She grabbed the coffee bag out of her knapsack, holding it in the air. "Coffee for peace?" The intensity of the situation hit them all at once, and despite the tension, they couldn't help but wonder, how? Marcus smiled and nodded his head. London agreed eagerly. "It's worth a shot!" With their makeshift plan in place, Marcus walked to the door, handing the bag to Fred. The aroma of coffee lingered in the air, an unexpected but potentially effective tool in their quest to speak to their extraterrestrial pursuers. Suddenly, red-jets began to land, perfectly in a single line.

"We were thinking... maybe we can negotiate with coffee?" Fred said as he handed Hue the bag. "Coffee for peace? Now that's a first." Said Hue. One of the red-cart jet doors open...a sharp and pristine swing. Silent and eerie. Two aliens began their descend, slowly touching the pink sand. Sort of thrown off by the color, they seemed to have an awkward walk. The aliens slowly approached the Hue as he held up the bag with a confidence stance. One alien, slightly taller and with a more intricate design on its suit, stepped forward and extended a long arm towards the jet. Hue took a deep breath and handed him the coffee bag. "We come in peace," he said, hoping the universal gesture of offering would be understood. The alien hesitated, its eyes scanning the bag curiously. It leaned in, taking a deep whiff of the aromatic coffee. A strange, guttural sound emanated from its chest, which Hue translated as a sign of approval. "Amazing" one alien said. "Amazing," the other alien said in a thick, halting accent, the syllables cracked but clear. The group froze. "Did... did he just speak English?" Tony whispered. Hue didn't miss a beat. "Maybe not English. Maybe mimicry." He lowered his tone. "Where do you come from?" The alien tilted his head, the glowing filaments along its face pulsing. "From... Sky," it answered slowly, the words grinding against its throat as if carved from stone. The smaller alien stepped closer, its movements smoother, more fluid. "From... far flame," it added, pointing upward toward the violet horizon where two suns overlapped faintly. "Stars," Anika whispered under her breath. "They're trying to say they come from the stars." Hue steadied him, his communicator training kicking in. "You... seek war, or peace?" he asked carefully, spacing out each word. The taller alien's glow dimmed, then pulsed again with a softer hum. "Peace... share." It tapped the coffee bag with a delicate motion, as though confirming the offering's meaning. "Share." London let out a sigh of relief. She clutched her chest. "We've just started the galaxy's first coffee trade deal." Marcus shot her a look but didn't hide the small smile tugging at his mouth. "Focus. If they're serious, this is bigger than us." The second alien crouched slightly, running its shimmering hand through the pink sand. "This..." it said, then gestured to the girls, then the boys. "This... same." "What's it trying to say?" asked Isabella. Hue narrowed his eyes, listening to the cadence of the guttural tones beneath the broken words. The alien's gaze turned back to Hue, eyes glowing faintly. "Teach," it said, the syllable clipped but purposeful. "Teach... peace." Anika inhaled sharply. "They don't just want coffee. They want us to teach them something. Or maybe they want to teach us." The taller alien straightened, the filaments along its torso shimmering brighter. It lifted the bag gently, holding it like a sacred artifact. "Coffee... peace. You... show." Hue's pulse raced. "They're asking us to prove it. To show what peace looks like." The group exchanged uncertain glances. Coffee had opened the door, but what came next would decide if that door led to an alliance, or something far more dangerous. Suddenly, Anika had a great idea. "London, quick. Let's make them a cup of coffee." Ivan chimed in, "that's a great idea."

Inside, the shipboard was sleek but functional, designed for efficiency, not comfort. Everything was modular: seats folded flush into the floor, storage compartments opened seamlessly from hidden panels, and a central table could retract into the deck when not in use. London hurried to the kitchen, pulling out another small pouch of ground coffee she had tucked into her knapsack back on Earth. The contrast was striking, her worn, Earth-made coffee bag against the pristine counters. "How is this a project?" She giggled. She opened a compartment, revealing a water reservoir already humming with filtered supply, changing her perception of water access. "Alright," she muttered, half to herself, half to the group, "let's hope coffee can be universal." Anika helped steady her as she set up, while Ivan located a coffee pot embedded into the counter's surface. It glowed faintly lavender as it activated, warming the small kettle London filled with water. The sound of steam filled the room, soft and familiar in the otherwise sterile ship.

The aroma began to rise, rich, earthy, unmistakable. It threaded through the ship's recycled air, breaking through the metallic tang of machinery and the sterile scent of filtration. Everyone paused, even the aliens outside. London carefully poured the hot water over the instant grounds in a mug she found nearby. She stirred gently, the sound of clinking metal oddly loud against the silence. The brew darkened quickly, releasing waves of comfort and familiarity. The liquid swirled inside, black and glossy as it settled, catching the ship's dim light. "Here it is," London whispered, clutching the cup. "Coffee for peace." Marcus stepped to the bay door, nodding for Hue to take the offering. Hue accepted the cup with steady hands, his heart racing. He glanced back at the group, seven sets of eyes filled with equal parts fear and hope, then turned to face the aliens waiting on the pink sand. The real test was about to begin.

5

Alien Alliance

Hue walked over and gently handed the cup to the taller alien. The two aliens shared the cup of coffee in silence. Hue nodded in understanding. "It's good." Then, without warning, the aliens began to speak to one another in rapid tones. The glowing filaments on their chests flashed in intricate patterns, fast, then slow, then pulsing in unison. Hue froze, straining to catch even a fragment of meaning, but the cadence was too complex. This wasn't mimicry, it was their language, alive and layered, a dialogue that none of them could break into. Th e group exchanged uneasy glances. London gripped her knapsack tighter, Anika leaned forward as though listening harder might unlock the code, and even Marcus's shoulders stiffened. Then, one of the aliens turned and walked back to its red-cart. The sleek craft opened, and the alien retrieved a round structure, a smooth vessel, shaped like a bowl yet glowing faintly from within. Liquid splashed inside, a pale oil that shimmered like mercury catching the light. Hue's eyes widened. His breath caught. "Oh no..." he whispered. "They're... they're offering something back." The taller alien approached, holding the vessel with both hands. It extended it toward Hue, its glowing chest dimming to a steady pulse as though waiting for a reply. Hue's throat tightened. Every instinct screamed don't. He had no idea what the liquid was, what it could do to him. Yet he could feel every pair of human eyes on him, the silent weight of their hope pressing against his hesitation.

"I don't..." he stammered, looking back at the group. "I'm not sure..." whispered Penn. "Mmmh," Marcus added, his voice firm but low. "They trusted us with their drink. Does it smell the same?" London quickly added, her voice steady despite her pale face. Hue leaned forward, exhaled slowly and took a swift. It smelled okay. His hand trembled as he reached out, the cool surface of the alien bowl slick against his fingers. The liquid rippled with strange colors almost reflecting the early morning sun. He raised it to his lips. His stomach clenched, but he closed his eyes and tipped the vessel back, letting the liquid slide across his tongue. It was unlike anything he had ever tasted, smooth, electric, almost humming as it spread across his mouth. It sent a warmth down his throat that flared into his chest, neither burning nor soothing, but alive. The aliens leaned closer, watching intently. Hue lowered the bowl, his face stoic and steady. He swallowed hard, then forced a small, shaky smile. "It's... good."

The aliens' filaments flared brighter, pulsing in perfect rhythm with one another. A new sound spilled from their throats. A low, resonant, and harmonious, like approval sung in chords. For the first time, it was clear: the exchange was complete. Coffee for peace. Drink for drink. And with it, the beginning of an alliance. Hue handed Frederick the bowl, "It only makes sense," said Hue as he processed what just happened.

Hue and Frederick began to have a conversation with the aliens as they enjoyed their drinks. Marcus, Ivan and Oksao approached Anika, London, and Penn with a mix of curiosity and concern on their faces. They had just witnessed an alien alliance for the first time in what they thought would be a life-or-death situation. But now they realized they knew very little about the girls and their situation. Marcus overheard Penn mentioning to Anika that they needed to get back to Bull Pin University. "Where is Bull Pin University?" Asked Marcus. "It's in Civilization 1," replied Penn. "We got knocked out of our wormhole while heading here. We need to get back as soon as possible. Our friends are counting on us to return," she finished. Wait, Civilization 1?" Ivan eyes widened. "Earth resides in Civilization 0. Our academy is specifically designed to train us in advanced technologies and strategies to elevate us to Civilization 1 status. Why'd you travel there?" Anika sighed. Her expression serious. "It's not that simple. Bull Pin University isn't just a place." "What is it?" asked Marcus. Anika hesitated, her eyes flicking toward London, then to Penn, as if searching for the right words. Finally, she exhaled.

"We were told that Bull Pin University isn't just a school. It's... a system. A place built after collapse, when the world had nothing left but scraps of survival. At first, it was meant to be an evolved establishment, a place where knowledge could be preserved. But it changed. It turned into something else." London's voice was still weak, but she added firmly, "It became a machine. Not just the robots, but the rules. Every lesson, every test, every moment inside those walls is measured. We're not people, we're data. They track our words, our steps, even our hesitations. Fail once, and you're labeled inefficient. Fail twice, and you're erased from the system completely." Marcus frowned, his brow tightening. "Erased? You mean expelled?" "No." Penn's voice was steady, but her eyes carried the weight of the truth. "Erased. It's why survival there isn't about creativity or growth. It's about obedience. Sufficiency. If you don't meet the system's standard, you don't belong in Civilization 1. And the cost of not belonging is..." She trailed off, letting the silence finish her sentence. Ivan's jaw clenched. "So they're filtering humanity. Stripping it down to what fits their design." "Exactly," Anika said. "Bull Pin University looks like progress from the outside, energy domes, endless resources, perfect climates. But inside, it's cold. It drains you. It decides who you are and what you're worth." Oksao shook his head, disbelief flickering in his eyes. "And you live in that? You train inside it?" London nodded. "We do more than that. We endure it. Because if we don't, we're gone. And yet... even within its walls, there are cracks. Robots like Crly are machines who are starting to see more than programming. People like us, who still believe in compassion, in faith, in something greater than sufficiency. That's what keeps us alive." The boys fell silent, their expressions shifting between shock and thought. Marcus finally broke it, his voice low. "Our academy's goal is to train us to be advocates for a Type 1 Civilization. To help rise there as proof of progress." Penn looked at him directly. For the first time, both groups realized they were standing on the same threshold. The alliance wasn't just with the aliens outside. It was forming between themselves, fragile but powerful, born out of a shared truth. Penn nodded at him solemnly, her gaze then fixed on the pink horizon.

6

Reunion in the Pink Desert

As the group began to settle down, Penn's eyes were fixed on the new eco-system and its engaging distractions. The sun shimmered perfectly against the sand, almost interacting with the grains, turning them tickled pink. The plants sunbathed in the distance, soaking up the last bit of shine that the day had to offer. And a rock nearby shined like glass, reflecting the sky off its back. She looked a bit closer at the rock and saw a dash glimmer across its home. Penn looked up and saw an object fly past them, raising an alarm that they have company. She looked over and saw Marcus staring at his dashboard, frozen but analyzing the situation with caution. "Company," Penn murmured. The aliens, once enemies but now uneasy allies, immediately shifted into formation, their sleek bodies angled in quiet defense. His hand hovered over the controls, ready yet cautious.

The sleek jet broke the horizon, the glow of its engines shimmering against the desert's shifting hues. London squinted. Her breath caught. "It's Crly?!" she exclaimed, her voice sharp with disbelief and hope. Anika's heart leapt. "Does that mean the others are with him?" she whispered, her pulse quickening. The ship drew closer, revealing familiar silhouettes framed in its windows, Crly at the front, with Kacey, Imon, Isabel, Tony, and a new girl, Dot, crowded behind him. Relief surged through the stranded group. Marcus guided their craft forward, signaling safety. The aliens relaxed, though their stance carried a reminder, friendship had its limits, and vigilance was survival.

The jets touched down on the soft pink sand. Doors swung open. In a rush of voices and movement, the groups collided into embraces. Tears, laughter, and disbelief mingled under the vast desert sky. Anika gripped Crly's arm tightly. "We thought we were lost," she admitted, her voice raw. Crly tilted his head, his mechanical features softened by something more human. "We never stopped searching." London stepped forward. Isabel's eyes went wide when she saw their new alien and male friends. Unsure about the recent history, she showed herself friendly. Dot's hands outstretched to meet them with a handshake. "Hi. Nice to meet you, I'm Dot," she said. Marcus nodded, shaking her hand with both hands warmly. The rest of the girls circled around, taking in the moment of time travel in disbelief as they marveled at their surroundings. For a fleeting moment, normalcy brushed against the chaos, soft coos, warm smiles, like friends reunited on foreign sand. But questions pressed in. Imon leaned close, her tone hushed but urgent. "So... who are they?" She glanced toward Marcus, Frederick, Ivan, Hue, Oksao and the watchful aliens beside them. Anika answered, steady. "We made it the hospital okay. I got the medication that I needed. But after the hospital, things spiraled. We were forced off course, crash-landed here, and met the guys.

This is Marcus, Frederick, Hue, Oksao and Ivan." Kacey took her time as she looked around the scene, searching for cues of a scratch on the ground. She picked up her head and blurted out, "You crash-landed?" Crly's protective instinct kicked in, and he began to circle the group, looking for signs of bruises or scratches. He lifted their arms and patted down their legs. Penn placed her hands out, placing them into Crly's wrists. "Yes," said Penn. "Well, not really a crash, it was like the sand knew we were coming and guided the jet down." Crly's wrist began to beep, indicating that Penn's temperature was a bit high. "You could probably use some water," he whispered to Penn. She nodded, grateful to have him around again. Penn turned around and started walking to the jet, starkly reminded that they needed to eat, drink, and sleep, especially in this new environment. Most of the girls were drained from the past few days. The excitement of it all captured their undivided attention.

Marcus moved out of the way as Penn headed back to the jet. His gentle concern for her was obvious, but he ignored it along with everything else that might have panned out as a distraction. "Hey, I'm Marcus," he said, reaching out for a handshake to the other girls. They were receptive. His presence was demanding yet calm. He patted his friends next to him on the back, introducing them one by one. The sun cast its shimmery light on the horizon as it slowly fell for the night. The rest of the evening was filled with an awkward moment of storytelling, while still getting to know the aliens. "Without them, we wouldn't have survived," Anika added with a wry half-smile. "Coffee diplomacy. Not conventional, but effective," Marcus added. A ripple of laughter eased the tension. Hue stepped in, voice calm but resolute. "They seem pretty open to helping us navigate this new environment and chart a safe way back home." The mood sobered. Kacey crossed her arms, her expression firm."

"Home?" she repeated. "That's a great point. Where is home for us now? Should we go back with them, or to Bull Pin University? We left right before it was time to take the exam... we figured it was better for them to come looking for us rather than take the exam without you three. We're so proud of you. I can't believe we were able to find you." Crly's optics flickered, his voice steady. "I tracked the jet using our satellite scanner, an energy tracker designed to read planetary output across layers of atmosphere." He paused, letting the weight of his words sink in. "It's my understanding that we live a Type 1 Civilization, we thrive on harnessing planetary energy itself. Every watt of light, every gust of wind, every fraction of heat is captured, stored, and gathered for efficiency. That's how I was able to follow your trail, the jet left a signature in the energy grid that no one else would notice. But it wasn't just technology. It was... clear you needed help. Your jet steered off chart. You gave me a reason to keep searching." The girls leaned closer, a mix of awe and unease on their faces. Imon's began to think out loud. "If that new society runs on total planetary control, then failure isn't just about an exam, it's about survival. We left to save ourselves, but maybe this is bigger than us." London, weary but thoughtful, finally spoke. "Maybe the question isn't whether we go back or move forward. Maybe it's whether we can create something different from the systems we've been trapped in. I mean, honestly, why go back to Bull Pin University?" The desert wind rustled, carrying silence over the group. For a moment, the stars above seemed sharper, colder...reminders of the civilizations beyond waiting to test them.

"Then we plan carefully. If we go back, it's not just survival, it's resistance." Tony nodded sharply. "We've faced too much to hesitate now. But rushing in unprepared is pointless." Silence fell, broken only by the aliens soft breathing. It was hard to tell if they were getting tired or restless. Still unsure of their new alien friends, they were unaware of how to deal with their proximity. Anika shifted uneasily, her gaze fixed on the aliens. She studied them from head to toe, unable to look away. Their skin was a dull, stone-grey, stretched smooth across tall, lean frames. From the sides of their heads protruded strange, tube-like ears that pulsed faintly as if catching every whisper of sound. The tight black spandex that clung to their bodies gave them an almost spectral appearance, both human and not, their movements too fluid, too deliberate. A shiver crawled up Isabella's spine. She couldn't tell if being so close to them was safe. Were they allies, or simply waiting for the right moment to reveal themselves as something else entirely? She folded her arms, forcing her expression to remain neutral, but her mind raced. Every subtle twitch, every glance from those alien eyes reminded her that this alliance was fragile, and trust was still far away. Isabella broke the silence and spoke what they all felt. "If we're going to change anything, we need more than courage. We need solid help." Marcus looked around, his voice carrying the weight of leadership. "Then that's our path. Train. Build alliances. When we return, we don't just go back, we go back strong enough to win." The group's agreement was wordless but firm, each nod sealing the unspoken pact. Then, the desert itself shifted. A nearby puddle shimmered, bubbling with iridescent light. Energy rippled across its surface until, with a sudden eruption, four figures tumbled out onto the sand. Lesly stood first, brushing pink grains from her orange outfit, her small curls dusted with glittering particles. "This gets easier every time," she muttered, offering a hand to Haisley, whose blonde ponytail was now streaked with sand. "Easier? We never land on our feet," Haisley groaned, tugging Sensi and Shon upright. Sensi's neat box braids framed her face, her olive-green eyes scanning warily, while Shon scowled, and her navy outfit streaked with dust. "Well, that was graceful," she said dryly. The astonished group stared. Shon raised her hands, half-apologetic, showing growth from her recent extraverted encounters. "Uh... hi. Sorry about the dramatic entrance. We didn't mean to crash your camp." Recovering her composure, she gestured to the others. "I'm Shon. This is Lesly, Sensi, and Haisley. We were... aiming for a ..." She took her time to think, deciding to not mention the map they were just given after leaving a nearby city. The four girls were from a nearby school named Smiley University. A new built structure that embodied the character of the Pink Desert and the ethos of its inhabitants. Their outfits were enriched with the culture that shimmered across the campus, perfectly fitting for their journeys that granted them access to distant locations.

A few days prior, Sensi, Lesly, Haisley, and Shon were living their ordinary island lives. Their small university was tucked away on the coast, the kind of place where everyone knew each other, and late-night walks meant the sound of waves brushing the shore more than the bustle of city streets. The girls' island wasn't just quiet beaches and crashing waves. At its center stretched a vibrant little city, alive with neon signs, painted walls, and markets that stayed open far past midnight. Narrow alleys glowed with electric blues and pinks, each corner offering food stalls, music, and the hum of scooters weaving through crowded streets. It was the kind of place where you could lose yourself in laughter, snacks in hand, while the night seemed to promise it would never end. That was the backdrop of their girls' night out. Spanish spilled between them as naturally as the music echoing from shopfronts, and the city lights made everything feel larger than life. For Sensi, Lesly, Haisley, and Shon, the city was taste of freedom, a burst of color and energy before returning to the seriousness of their volleyball training. The stretch end of the night weighed heavy on their energy, blending together the colors and music alike. A large shimmering shadow dashed by their peripheral view, causing them to pause in their tracks. It was Archie.

His wings shimmered like a neon lantern brought to life, he didn't feel out of place in their world. He looked like another strange decoration of their glowing streets. Drinks slipped from their hands, laughter turned to shouts, and in chasing him they tore down the very alleys they had wandered so many nights before. Only this time, the city's lights bent into something more, a glowing portal waiting to transport them to the home of Smiley University. The pink shimmer spat them out into a landscape unlike anything their island city could have prepared them for. The ground beneath their feet glowed with pale pink sand that seemed alive, pulsing faintly like a heartbeat. Above them, the sky stretched in soft bands of turquoise and violet, a sun hanging low and heavy with a red-orange tint. The first shock wasn't just the scenery, it was themselves. Their clothes had changed. Where there had been casual outfits from a night out, they now wore sleek uniforms, each designed as if it were tailored to their personalities and strengths. The fabric clung and shimmered, almost humming with energy. "¿Qué es esto?" Lesly whispered, tugging at her new gear. Haisley raised her arm, gasping as arcs of light sparked faintly from her fingertips. "Is that, electricity? Coming out of my hands?" Her voice cracked between fear and awe. Sensi glanced around, wide-eyed, and spotted Archie hovering ahead, wings glowing brighter than before. "There he is!" Before they could argue, the air shifted. A low vibration ran through the ground, and in the distance, clear glittery water pools shimmered like gateways themselves. Shon crouched down, curiosity overtaking her fascination with Archie. "How weird," she murmured, hovering her finger over the shimmering water, which released a lukewarm wave heat across her finger tip. But when she tried to pull back, her hand wouldn't budge. She gave an empirical. "I can't get out!" The others grabbed for her, each pulling in desperation, but the pool surged like it had its own will. One tug turned into a tumble, and all four were yanked forward together, their screams muffled as the pool swallowed them whole. With a violent burst of light, the girls were spat out onto solid ground. They rolled across polished sand, coughing, dizzy, and disoriented. Their eyes blinked against the impossible pink light until it finally settled around them, warm and soft like a sunrise that refused to end.

"¿Qué fue eso?" Lesly gasped, sitting up and shaking glittering grains from her short curly hair. The sand shimmered under her hands, each particle glowing faintly as if it were alive. Haisley groaned beside her, flipping onto her back. "No tengo idea, pero si esto es un sueño... por favor que alguien me despierte ya." Sensi gasped breathlessly, brushing sand from her cheeks. "Mira esto, ¡es rojillo! ¿Estamos en una playa o en una pintura?" said Sensi. "Parece algodón de azúcar," Shon said, her voice still trembling with adrenaline. "Pero no es caliente...pero mira, un desert." said Shon. She pressed her palm down and the sand pulsed faintly in response, like a soft heartbeat beneath her hand. They stared at it, mesmerized, then burst out laughing again, half nerves, half disbelief. "Esto no puede ser real," Lesly said, pushing herself to her feet. Her new uniform caught the light, a sleek orange suit with gold seams that gleamed whenever she moved. "Chicas... nuestras ropas. ¿Qué nos pasó?" Sensi turned in a slow circle, inspecting her own tan and green outfit. "No sé, pero esto parece sacado de una película de ciencia ficción." She tugged at the fabric. "Y se siente... vivo." Haisley examined her brown collar, the fabric sparking faintly at her fingertips. "No, en serio. Esto está loco. Hace cinco minutos estábamos comiendo helado y hablando del partido de voleibol..." said Haisley.

"¡El partido!" Shon yelled suddenly, hands flying to her head. "El juego! Se supone que jugábamos esta mañana." The group froze, the realization hitting all at once. "¿Y si ya empezó?" Lesly asked, panic creeping into her tone. "¿Y si nos descalifican?" Sensi replied quickly. "¿Y si mi mamá se entera?" Haisley groaned. "Va a matarme. ¡Nos va a matar a todas!" They all spoke over each other, voices rising in overlapping chaos. "¿Dónde está mi teléfono?" Shon patted her sides frantically, then looked up, horrified. "No traje el bolso. ¡Lo dejé en la casa!"

"Yo también," Lesly admitted, checking her empty pockets. "Genial. Perfecto." Said Sensi. The four stood in silence for a beat, staring at one another. Then Haisley exhaled and kicked at the sand. "¿Y si caminamos hacia allá?" She pointed toward a glowing sign in the distance where the pink ground shifted into lavender tones. "Tal vez haya una carretera o algo." Lesly frowned. "¿Carretera? No hay ni una nube, ni edificios... ni nada." Sensi squinted toward the horizon. "Pero hay algo allá." She pointed. In the distance, the sky swirled like a soft cinnamon swirl mirage. There was a faint glimmer of movement. "Parece una cancha de voleibol," Shon said, squinting. "No puede ser..." The others followed her gaze and there it was. The dunes sloped downward into what looked unmistakably like a court, only this one shimmered in shades of pink and purple. Two crystalline poles framed a net made of light, and hovering just above the surface was a glowing ball, suspended midair as if waiting for them. The girls fell silent. "Esto no puede ser coincidencia," Lesly said finally, her voice barely a whisper. "Es... hermoso," murmured Sensi. "Y completamente imposible," Haisley added. They stared for a long moment, torn between awe and disbelief. Lesly swallowed hard. "¿Y si no podemos volver?" Sensi looked at each of them, then at the floating volleyball gleaming like a tiny sun. "Entonces jugamos," she said softly, her lips curling into a nervous smile. For a heartbeat, no one moved. Then laughter returned, hesitant, unsure, but real. The kind of laughter that only comes when fear and wonder collide. "Está bien," Haisley said, shaking her head as she bent to scoop the glowing ball from the sand. "Pero si esto cuenta como práctica, quiero puntos extras." The pink desert stretched endlessly around them, silent except for the echo of their voices, carried by a wind that almost sounded like applause. Glittering sand clung to their new uniforms as they staggered towards the court, trying to make sense of the towering structure before them. As they came closer, an archway stretched above, its name spelled in bold in shimmering letters, "Smiley University." Still catching their breath, they dusted themselves off, exchanging wide-eyed looks of disbelief.

They walked up to the gated structure in caution and the court looked even larger up close. It stood next to what looked like a red-glass arena. Its windows stretched from bottom to top, and the building lacked corners, making a complete circle. Then, from behind a rock formation at the gate, shadows stirred. Figures stepped into view. Other students in uniforms glowing with strange colors and patterns. And then, one broke away to speak. A tall figure with bright yellow hair and a matching yellow outfit approached. Her steps were confident and voice steady. "Welcome," said the girl in the yellow. The four girls froze.

7

It's Training Time

The plaza outside the red-glass arena was a living river and students in sleek uniforms flowed toward the glass doors in tight lines, while staff in bright vests kept order with crisp hand gestures. "Single file to enter the building! We need your training pass and your IDs to compete today. If you're just here to watch, please enter through the other side door," said a woman professor with bright pink hair and a clipboard tucked under her arm. Lesly slowed to a stop. The city's grit was still on her shoes; the desert's glitter still clung to her sleeves. "No tenemos nada," murmured Sensi. "Not a pass... not even a name for this place." Sensi followed her gaze up the tiers of red glass. From somewhere high, a band warmed up, the sound thin and metallic against the building's curve. She caught a flicker of violet in her periphery. It was Archie, skimming a banner before vanishing behind a column. "I bet they know what's going on," she said, chin tipping toward a group of varsity students in matching jackets moving with practiced ease, the kind of people who never had to guess where to stand.

Haisley, still buzzing from the electricity that had crackled at her fingertips, exhaled and stepped out of the stream of people in line. "Excuse me," she asked a student who'd paused to scan her wristband at a pillar. "What is everyone training for?" The girl, pale-haired with a soft scarf looped twice at her throat and bright star stickers all over her cheeks, which looked like freckles, looked surprised only for a beat, then smiled like this was the best week of the year. "Hey. You must be new...my name is Freckles. It's finals week," she said. "Fortissimo is here." Shon blinked. "Fortissimo... like a team?" "Yes, a Galatic varsity team," the girl corrected, eyes bright. "They come in to push us. If you're competing, you'll know. If you're not..." She nodded toward a side entrance marked spectators. "...you should probably head to that line," said Freckles. The four exchanged a look. The professor walked by again, ushering a new wave toward the crowd. "Competition line to your left." she said. Sensi tugged at the cuff of her uniform. The fabric answered with a faint hum, as if aware of her pulse. "We don't have IDs" she whispered. "We need answers," Haisley whispered back as she pressed her palm to the glass pillar.

Lesly tracked the crowd. The way teams moved like single bodies, the way captains never broke stride, the way the lost were gently diverted toward their place. The whole place ran on quiet rules. "Ask another person," Shon said. "Look! Over there," Shon said. The trio in warm-yellow uniforms stood near a stone outcrop, their conversation easy and unhurried despite the flow. Leaders. Or at least they treated them like it. They threaded through, careful not to break formation as lines re-stitched around them. The four girls drew closer, to meet the same bright-haired figure who'd greeted them at the gate. Sensi gently tapped the familiar girl's shoulder, grabbing her attention. "Welcome," she said again, this time with a hint of recognition. "We don't have ID," Sensi said before nerves could crowd her throat. "No training pass. We're not... from here." Sensi replied. "That much I gathered. My name is Sasha." Her smile was quick, not unkind. They tipped their head toward Archie, who had reappeared and now hovered just above the arch-way like a violet punctuation mark. "Are we in trouble if we don't have one?" Lesly asked. "Only if you block the competition queue. Come with me." They cut along the arena's curve, past a mural of past champi-ons. Rows of faces rendered in clean lines and hard light, into the shelter of an overhang where the noise thinned. They passed through the building, down a hallway, which led them to the outside court filled with teams that were busy practicing. From here, the arena's heartbeat was more obvious. The call-and-response horns, the crisp thud of practice lollipops, and the high bright chatter of teams psyching themselves up.

"Fortissimos," Sasha said, watching a wall display cycle through brackets. "They're here to close our season. They don't ease anyone in." said Sasha. "What exactly are you training for...and how do you train?" Haisley asked. "To be in control," Sasha said. "Of our abilities and better teamwork." Their eyes flicked to Haisley's fingers, as if they could still see the faint spark she'd coaxed without trying. Shon folded her arms. "What do you mean by our abilities?" "That depends," Sasha said. She tapped a small advanced sleek slate-like watch on her wrist. A panel slid open revealing a narrow reception desk with a single attendant behind it on the 3D screen. The attendant's expression said they had seen every ability and filed it by levels. "Intake can issue temporary observer bands. That gets you in the building, not on a floor. You'll be tested, lightly. You'll need your ID to explain what they expect of you. But you should be okay. We typically don't throw people into finals week." The professor's voice lifted again across the plaza, cheerful and strict at once. Lines tightened. The sound of a whistle cut cleanly. Somewhere, a door thudded shut like a starting noise.

Sensi traded a look with the others. Island night, neon alleys, glitter pools, everything had been a cascade. This, at least, felt like a choice. "Where are the bands," she said. Archie drifted down, settled for a second on the stone, and pulsed his wings like he approved. You can grab them here, pointing at a what looked like a pull-down table. It had a sleek screen neatly placed above it, with an intake survey form on its interface. Sasha slid her finger across the screen and its welcome sign floated across the screen in multicolor fashion. "Place your finger on the screen," said Sasha. Lesly went first. Her blue-orange suit shimmered in the light, leaving a sparkle that chased her. The screen took its time as it read her finger prints. "Telekinesis," Sasha murmured, eyes widening as the diagnostic symbols spun faster. "Control over objects and the ability to move them." The light snapped off, leaving only Lesly's reflection staring back. Sasha's wrist was still perfectly placed in an angle to interact with the attendant on her phone. The attendant behind the desk lifted their brow. "That's not beginner level," she said quietly. Lesly drew her hand back. The air trembled where she'd touched it, as though the world itself was still adjusting to the idea of her. "What does that mean?" said Lesly. Sasha pointed to a court nearby. It was neatly placed behind the circular red building, with a large cage in the center form. "You'll practice over there, with the Junior Varsity team." A small laminated badge popped out of the machine with her name printed on top. Below it read her ability information alongside their expectations. It glowed softly, her name etched across the top, followed by a line of text that read "Ability is telekinesis. Expectation is controlled precision."

Lesly read the text out loud, shocked by the information. She was unfamiliar with telekinesis, let alone controlled precision. "How am I supposed to learn this?" Sasha took the card from her hand and pointed to the corner of the tag. "Place this code against your suit and you'll feel the tension to pursue the ability." She took a closer look at the ID and saw strange symbols in an unfamiliar pattern. She took a moment to think and then lifted against her shoulder, assured that she would at least have self-awareness of its reaction. She felt a slight tingle the sides of her suit arm and legs, and then a cool brush against her finger tips. The card immediately was rejected from her hands across the desert floor. "Woah!" yelled Shon. "Look at it go," said Haisley. Sensi was sold. "I'm next," she said confidently. She walked past the other two yellow suited guides and straight to the machine. She placed her finger over the scanner in hopes of something that matched her personality. "Light Refraction," Sasha read. "Bends visibility, seen when she wants to be and invisible when she doesn't." Sensi stuck her hands out in front of her and held them up to the sun. Her body seemed to be the same. She wasn't sure how that was even possible. The card spat out her ID and she quickly got a hold of it. She placed it in front of her shoulder, in wonder of their new environment. "How is this possible?" she looked down and noticed that her feet began to blend with the sand. "Incredible" Haisley whispered. "That's interesting," Sasha whispered. "Is light refraction Junior Varsity, Ann?" she yelled out to her friend. Ann shrugged her shoulders. Sasha looked down at her wrist, the attendant typing at the speed of light. "No...not according to the list." Said the assistant. "Didn't we see a Fortissimos girl do light refraction last year?" The light from Sasha's watch glowed against her stickers as the assistant talked. "Yes!" said Loral, the girl standing next to Ann. "So, if I'm not in Junior Varsity, where do I go?" Sensi was confused. "You belong in Varsity," Loral said. She smiled and pointed to the other court with an extra-large cage on the court. There was a giant cotton candy lollipop on the top of the building. Sensi shook her head in compliance, as if she were just recruited for the varsity volleyball team.

"What about me?" said Shon. She stepped up to the machine and put her finger on the screen. Sasha leaned in again, offering the same support to her new peer. They paused, eyeing the screen for an explanation. "Teleportation!" claimed Sasha. The card spat straight out like a lotto machine, charging Shon to her new team. "That's Varsity!" said Loral, excited to point her along. Shon placed her tag against her shoulder, curious to see if she felt different from before. She felt a quick jolt against her body, as she suddenly moved 5 feet forward. "Woah!" said Shon. "So, is this what happened earlier when I stuck my finger in the water?" she said. "What do you mean?" said Sasha. "There was a large, slightly steamy puddle in the desert, when we first arrived. It was so beautiful. I've never seen anything like it and I tried to touch it. I couldn't pull my finger out and they tried to help by pulling me out." said Shon. "Did you fall in?" questioned Sasha. "It felt like I was grabbed in." she said. "That's strange..." said Loral. "Maybe it was a reaction to your ability," said Haisley, "I want to go next."

Haisley stepped forward, excitement already building in her chest. The machine hummed faintly, recognizing the shift in presence as she placed her fingers on the scanner. The light from the machine pulsed. Sasha leaned closer, brows knitting. "That's... new." The attendant looked up. "Multicolored lightning manipulation," Haisley and Sasha said slowly, as if reading them carried a charge of their own. "Generates and controls lightning in varied colors, each with unique capabilities." Haisley leaned back. "What does that even mean?" she asked, half in awe. The ID slid out of the slot and she caught it midair, her name glowing faintly across the top. Sasha smiled, shaking her head slightly. "Varsity," she confirmed while looking at her assistant.

Haisley rotated her wrist, and the faintest arc of turquoise lightning curved between her fingers, flickering before disappearing completely. "Each color feels... different," she said, the wonder in her voice unmistakable." Haisley said, her pulse racing. She looked toward the practice courts where Lesly's telekinetic movements were beginning to take form and Sensi shimmered faintly in and out of sight. They each grabbed a lanyard from the ID machine and snaped on their IDs to the plastic clip. "Welcome to Smiley University," Sasha said alongside Lorel and Ann. It was their third time saying it, and now it sounded less like hospitality and more like the start of a test.

Meanwhile at Fortissimos

Civilization 4 was alive with rhythm. From orbit, the planet itself shimmered like a vinyl disc spinning in deep space. Its crescent moon shaped like a music note, glowing orange against an indigo sky. Every gust of wind carried a harmony. Every light pulse was part of a larger tempo. The world sounded alive and it was. The city of Fortissimos, capital and heart of the civilization, stood as a testament to the pluralism sonic engineering. Its buildings were cybernetic instruments made of flutes and violins fused into glass towers, brass domes humming with low tones, and streets that resonated faintly when walked upon, each step triggering a hidden note beneath the surface. Public transit moved not on rails or wheels, but on vibrational frequencies, gliding across magnetic sound waves that kept the air in constant song. In this world, music wasn't art, it was energy. Frequency was power. Melody was identity. Every citizen's heartbeat aligned with the city's central beat, and every resonance was recorded in crystalline panels known as "Sound Archives," preserving the harmonics of history itself.

Amid the grand orchestral hum stood three of Fortissimos' most gifted students Courtesy, Yola, and Haven, the trio whose talents had earned them the honor of representing Civilization 4 in inter-civilization trials, aka finals week. Together, they were known simply as the varsity team that came to challenge Smiley's Varsity team.

The four girls prepared for their send off in their musical high-tech classroom. Clad in her bright orange uniform, Courtesy's presence was impossible to ignore. With a flick of her hand, she could bend air into rhythm, shaping invisible sound waves like sculpted glass. Her gift, Sound Manipulation, allowed her to create, weaponize, or silence frequencies across any medium including air, water, even solid ground. She could amplify whispers into sonic booms, turn silence into a crushing vacuum, or destabilize molecules with resonant vibration. "Control the resonance, don't let it control you," her mentor always said. Courtesy smiled faintly because control had never been her problem. Restraint was. Next to her stood Yola, calm and analytical, dressed in sleek gray armor that pulsed faintly with every sound wave she released. Her ability, *Echolocation,* allowed her to see without sight, emitting sound waves that bounced back as perfect mental blueprints of her surroundings. No invisibility, camouflage, or illusion could deceive her. She could track footsteps through concrete, sense heartbeats through walls, and identify weaknesses in structures by analyzing the vibrations in their frames. To Yola, the world was a constant dialogue of echoes and truth spoken through frequency. Her every breath returned with data. Every movement mapped in the silent symphony of space. Finally, there was Haven, radiant in pink, her expression serene and her posture composed. Her voice carried more than beauty, it carried power. With Singing Mastery, Haven possessed perfect pitch, infinite range, and flawless control over tone, rhythm, and emotion. Her songs could calm chaos, rally crowds, or reshape morale itself. When she sang, the atmosphere shifted and pressure changed, air thickened, and listeners found their emotions rewired. Her melodies could lull enemies into stillness or awaken allies to courage. During training, her song Harmony Pulse had synchronized an entire city's power grid and every light blinking to her tempo. "Your voice demands control," Yola once told her. "Control," Haven replied, "when necessary."

The three stood on a vast amphitheater terrace, the planet's metronome tower ticking faintly in the distance. They had just completed their morning run for the day, which included a light warm up and studying with their favorite cup of coffee. Their professor, Corva, approached them. Her coat lined with sound-reactive fibers that rippled with every step. "Ladies," she began, her voice echoing across the terrace with harmonic precision, "you've mastered the tempo of this semester. Now, you'll face the testing of another." She gestured to a portal ring tuned to a frequency outside their known range. The air shimmered like rippling sheet music. "Civilization 3 awaits and Smiley University is waiting for you. Remember, they will not hear you as you are here. You must tune yourselves to their world." Courtesy rolled her shoulders, Yola adjusted her hairband, and Haven's hum whispered softly a perfect C note that steadied the air. Their confidence took over the room. As the portal opened, the moon's note-shaped reflection shimmered above them. Their world's symphony swelled and strings, brass, and percussion interlocking in perfect crescendo as the Fortissimos stepped forward into finals week.

Finals Week at Smiley University

The portal flared open above the red-glass arena, spilling Courtesy, Yola, and Haven into the heart of Smiley University. Silence rippled through the plaza as the trio landed with practiced ease, their uniforms glowing faintly with harmonic resonance. The Varsity courts came alive and students paused mid-warm-up, brackets flickered across the wall displays, and whispers spread, "Fortissimos had arrived." The Smiley girls watched wide-eyed from their training circle. Shon, Lesly, Haisley and Sensi had just begun to learn about their new abilities when the Fortissimos emerged like living music. Smiley didn't know it, but Fortissimos was there to make music. It That was why Civilization 4 was considered advanced. Their cities ran on tuned air, their transit on resonance, their movements on echo. Music there wasn't art; it was infrastructure. Sasha lifted a hand and sent Yellow Varsity to a side court to warm up against the visitors later. The four newcomers stayed at the rail, watching and not competing. The crowd pressed closer, bodies knitting into a bright ring around both teams. The pressure of eyes, the heat, the low murmur captured Shon, Lesly, Haisley, and Sensi's attention as they edged back, step by careful step. Haven lifted her chin and let out a deep, carrying yell. It wasn't anger, but a tuning call. The sound hit the rafters, slid down the red glass, and pushed a broad pressure front across the court. Air cooled as it expanded; the resonance scraped moisture from the ceiling seams and the arena opened its sky. First a deep thunderous sound, then a sheet of rain. It hammered the glass and kissed the floor, beading, running, pooling in multicolored droplets. "Haisley!" Sensi started. "I know," Haisley breathed. Turquoise charge gathered along her forearms, the rain beading into lines of light. Static rain crackled. A warm puddle rolled to Shon's shoe, steaming faintly on the heated court. She felt the catch in her gut and it was the same latch as before. "Hold on!" she said, already reaching for them. Lesly's grip closed around her wrist; Sensi's fingers locked over Lesly's; Haisley's spark stitched them together. Shon wasn't sure how to control it yet, but she knew they were teleporting to their next location. The arena blinked, and the spot where they'd stood was empty.

Pocketed Dunes

They reappeared on the far side of the desert, the rain thinning to mist, the sky wide and restless. A woman in glasses walked toward them from a scatter of low, modern homes that dotted the dunes like lanterns. As she drew close, the lantern light showed the seams of her transparent skin. A soft geometry danced against the framework of her body. Dust slid through her sleeve and bent the glow from the lanterns reflections. "Don't be afraid," she said, voice warm and a half-beat delayed. "I'm the caretaker here," her warm smile drawing them in, "And by the looks of it, one of you transported here accidently, I'm guessing." Shon stood up, dusting off her outfit and let off a slight blush. "Yes, that would be me," she said as she helped the rest of her friends. "You're not from this pocket," the woman said gently. "No," said Sensi, "how do we get back?" Sensi's stomach let out a loud rumble, reminding the girls that they needed food...and probably shelter. "My name is LB," said the woman as she took in their situation. "When the power holds, I can cook you a meal." She glanced at the flickering lights reflecting in the window of her home. "How do you fix the power?" Lesly asked. "They're called Pink Coins," LB said with kindness. "There's a natural run of them out on the flatlands, near the plant fields equilibrium. Excuse me, I'll be right back with some water." She motioned them to wait, then returned with four battered water bottles. "Drink," she said as she handed them each a water. Shon didn't move. "Water..." she said softly. "It's how I...lose control." LB studied her. "It didn't take you. You answered it. Water strengthens your signal; when you're scared, you overcast your ability." She lifted Shon's hand and curled her fingers around the bottle. "Sip. Tell it you're staying." Shon took a careful drink. Nothing shifted. Her shoulders lowered.

LB continued, "You're in Civilization 3 now. We travel by the nature itself. Water can be a catalyst, among other things. You must learn yourself first alongside ecosystem." She stepped to the doorway, drew a quick map, and handed it to Shon. "Here, the directions to flatlands by the plant fields. Pink coins surface there after heat cycles within the pink sand. They're stunning. Sort of hard to miss. All you have to do is dig for them. They usually spat out towards the surface once they're done forming." LB tapped the circle, then pointed to Shon's ID. "Press it to your shoulder and think about this map." Shon pressed the badge to her suit; a faint hum answered. "Three steps," LB said. "Breath. Anchor. Link. Breathe steady. Anchor to the circle on this map, hold it in your mind until it feels like home. Then link hands so the earth knows who to carry." They moved to the threshold. Lesly took Shon's left hand; Sensi gripped Lesly's; Haisley slid in on Shon's right, a pale thread of turquoise sparking across their knuckles. "On your exhale," LB coached.

Shon closed her eyes mustering up her interdependence, and the other girls placed their hands against her shoulder. The circle on the map bloomed behind her lids. Flatlands, plant rows like stitches, a low rise in the distance. The sand under their boots cooled, then warmed. The world tipped once, clean, gentle, and folded. They landed on packed, wind-combed pink sand ground. Ahead stretched the plant fields, their rows rippling in the breeze; at their edges, the sand glittered from the pink coins half-bloomed from the flats like pebbles in glass. Voices lifted among their awkward entrance. Heads turned, while Anika, London, Penn, Marcus and the rest had widening eyes. Four figures stood from a shimmer and waved, relief breaking like sunrise. The night was late but youthful...awaiting long introductions and explanations of newly found civilizations.

8

Coins

By morning, everyone knew everyone else's story. The morning was filled with exhaustion, as they caught as much sleep as they could. Conversation filled the night, where sleep should have been. Most of the group agreed they would go back and help Bull Pin University. First, though, Shon, Lesly, Haisley, and Sensi would return to the pocketed city to bring LB the coins she needed to power her home. Thinking about LB's home, Lesly sparked the first conversation for the morning "What's for breakfast?"

They raided what they could from the Bear Pin and Bull Pin jets, ration packs, a dented kettle, a travel press, and enough food to feed the group comfortably. Coffee bloomed in the cold air. Dark, steadying and symbol of recent peace. Breakfast was whatever they could warm on portable coils: flat cakes, protein strips, and a tiny tin of sweet potato paste. For a few minutes, the world was quiet. Then the weather found them. The line of clouds that had been brooding at the horizon shouldered closer. Wind lifted the pink sand like sheets and its grit whispered along the hills. The four Smiley girls ducked into the jet entry, unsettled by the way weather kept approaching them. Archie fluttered near the hatch, his metallic wings refracting the storm's violet light. He gave a soft pulse, almost like a warning, before retreating under the wing of the jet.

As Shon turned to pull the hatch, something flashed at the threshold, barely there, then gone. Lesly caught it. "Wait," she said. "There." Half buried in the sand she saw a pink coin, the same impossible hue as the sand. It would have vanished again, but the wind rolled a thin skin of moisture over it and the coin held the light differently, like glass with a pulse. Haisley crouched. "No wonder we couldn't find any. They're really the same color as everything else. It would have taken us days to find one without the wind." London slid closer, eyes narrowing. "Did the woman, LB, say anything else? Why are these so important to power her home?" Shon shrugged her shoulders, "She said that they grow naturally out here." Sensi, Anika and Crly headed towards the coin. "She also said we can travel by the nature itself. It has something to do with the ecosystem." Sensi picked up the coin and handed it to Anika. Crly studied the glimmering surface. "If these coins hold power, or at least part of the landscape's energy, then LB's home might not just be powered by them. It might be part of the same system. The coins store what the land releases," he said, turning the coin slightly so its reflection pulsed across his hand. "When the wind moves through the sand, it stores energy. The coins absorb that charge and hold it like a battery. That's why they're the same color as the sand, they're born out of it." Crly handed Anika the coin, and she turned the coin over in her hand, watching the light shift across its edge. "So, the weather powers them? Not the Sun?" she said in amazement. "Essentially," That's how LB's house stays running, she's tapped into the planet itself." Anika nodded slowly. "So how many do you think there are?" She said. Marcus jumped up from his makeshift sit from having breakfast. "Thousands, maybe more," Marcus said, his voice rising over the wind. "If the whole desert's producing them, they probably run the entire city."

Ivan stood up. "Or maybe they're rare. She said she needed just a handful to power her home. If that's true, one coin might be worth more than the jet itself." Hue leaned against the hull, squinting into the shifting sand. "We could bring one back and try to test one." Haisley frowned remembering that they also had a home outside of the Pink Desert. The storm's hum deepened, wrapping around their voices. Somewhere in the distance, the four alien jets flickered in and out of the haze, its figures still inside, silhouettes shifting behind the tinted glass. Archie hovered beside the group, scanning the distant skies that reflected the gentle orange smokey haze. He let out a faint trill, half-question, half-signal, as if to confirm the strangers were still non-hostile.

They hadn't left since the night before. One of them raised a slender arm, pointing toward the group, and the others turned in unison. No words reached them, but their movements had a rhythm, measured, almost conversational. They were watching the commotion regarding the Pink coin. "Great," Shon muttered. "We've got an audience," she said, still not use to their presence. Sensi exhaled, steadying her tone. "Ignore them. Oksao said that they're friendly." She stepped forward, while helping Imon up. "We'll need more if we're bringing power back to LB. Shon, Haisley, Marcus, you head east toward the mountains. Ivan, London, Anika, Crly and I'll go south toward the flats. I guess everyone else, you stay here and collect whatever the storm uncovers." The group seemed to be growing the day. The excitement of getting to know each other almost overpowered the mood of their new pink coin gold rush. Lesly glanced toward the sky, where streaks of violet light were beginning to crawl between the clouds, starkly reminded of their new found abilities. She adjusted her ID which gently layed across her neck and looked toward the horizon, where the wind kept curling pink sand into rings. "Before we start looking," she said, "maybe we should talk about what we can actually do. If these coins are part of the landscape, maybe our abilities can help us find them faster." The group quieted, their attention shifting as if reminded that their powers weren't just skills, they were survival tools now. Lesly's question lingered, and for a moment, no one moved. Then Sensi glanced toward the horizon, the light from the clouds faintly reflecting in her visor. "LB told us something before we left," she said, her tone thoughtful. "She said control doesn't start with ability, it starts with thought." "In what way?" Ivan walked over and asked. Sensi drew a slow breath. "She said the mind decides before the power ever does. If your thoughts scatter, your control scatters with them. Out here, the land mirrors whatever you're feeling. Fear, doubt, anger...it all gets amplified." Shon looked down at the sand under her boots. "I understood it the same way," she said quietly. "When I'm panicking, I end up in a random place. But when I clear my head, it's like the space just opens for me." Lesly nodded. "I think this can be applied telekinesis. I can't move anything until I try to control it. The second I relax, things start gently moving. I noticed this when I first got my ID." Haisley's voice came from behind them, calm but curious. "So... focus and emotion have to balance." "Exactly," Sensi said. "LB said the real danger isn't losing power, it's losing direction. The stronger the thought, the stronger the outcome." All of the girls from Bull Pin University listened, arms crossed, a little uncertain. Their training had always been structured and precise, textbook-driven. They hadn't been taught to feel their way through anything. Power, to them, came through study, not instinct.

Isabella broke the silence first. "We weren't trained like that," she admitted. "At Bull Pin, everything was measurable by cause, effect and equation. We followed data, not feelings." Kacey adjusted the cuff of her sleeve, nodding slightly. "Our instructors said emotion clouds judgment. The only way to master technology was to strip out the human part of it." Imon frowned. "But that's the flaw, isn't it? LB sounds like she's teaching you how to connect with what you control, not just operate it." Anika nodded, glancing down at the coin in her hand. "Exactly. LB said the mind and matter respond to each other. It's not about command, it's about cooperation." Isabella folded her arms tighter. "Still... I don't know how that works for us. We didn't come out here with powers. We came out here with protocols." Sensi looked at her gently. "Then maybe this place is what changes that. The desert doesn't care who trained you...so far it reacts to who you are." Crly, standing just behind them, spoke up, his voice even and deliberate. "You're both correct. Bull Pin University taught control through logic, but teachings here seem to be about control through consciousness. Civilization 3 was designed to merge both approaches. Mind and system. Emotion and reason. One without the other collapses under stress." Crly's words hung there, steady as the hum of the jet. For a moment, no one spoke. Then Imon looked toward him, curiosity sharpening her voice. "So, if Civilization 3 merges both, where does that leave Civilization 1?" Crly's sensors flickered softly. "Civilization 1 has created an interesting foundation. A society built on precision and fear of inefficiency. Everything had to be justified by numbers. They believed progress only came from measurement and outcome." London crossed her arms, her expression thoughtful. "Every move monitored, every task logged. It wasn't just about learning, it was about proving worth." Anika tilted her head. "It seems like Civilization 1 mistook silence for stability. When people stopped questioning, the system thought it was succeeding." Isabella gave a faint, ironic smile. "That sounds about right," she said, "creativity was treated like static. Something to filter out." Sensi looked between them, her tone softer. "But that's why we need both. Civilization 1 built the system; Civilization 3 learns how to breathe inside it." Crly nodded. "Exactly. Civilization 1 perfected control. Civilization 3 redefines it. One focuses on order, the other on awareness." Kacey exhaled slowly. "So maybe what we're learning now isn't new. It's the evolution of what we already knew. Civilization 1 gave us structure, but this place...challenges our purpose." The guys were silent...not sure when to step in.

The guys were silent, unsure when to step in. For a moment, the hum of the alien jet filled the quiet, low and rhythmic, like it was waiting too. Then Marcus cleared his throat, his voice steady but reflective. "You're right about control and awareness," he said. "But for us, it's different. We came from a Type 0 Civilization, with aspirations of becoming a Type 1 Civilization. Bear Pin wasn't built for consciousness or emotion. It was built for order in chaos. Everything was about preparation." Ivan nodded. "We were trained for the threshold. The moment when systems start to fail, and humanity has to choose whether to evolve or collapse. That's what Bear Pin specialized in. Propulsion, crisis mapping, communication across unstable environments. We were supposed to keep humanity from breaking apart, by becoming a Type 1 Civilization." Hue leaned against the hull, his gaze steady on the sand. "But no one told us what happens when control isn't enough. We learned how to respond, not how to feel. Every action had a chart, every outcome had a probability. It made us efficient." Archie fluttered above the parting teams, orbiting once before settling between them, his wings catching the violet sky like glass. For a moment, his low hum connected both groups, a reminder that even in separation, they were still being watched over.

Oksao adjusted a panel on his wristband, its faint light flickering. "At Bear Pin, tech wasn't just a tool, it was identity. They said as long as we could calculate, we could survive. But that only works when the problem's mechanical." Frederick gave a small nod. "Exactly. We were right at the transition point. Ready to build something new but still afraid to let go of the old. Civilization 1 is supposed to start with us." Sensi tilted her head. Marcus looked at the coin still in Anika's palm. The wind swept through the clearing, carrying fine trails of sand around their boots. The conversation fell quiet again, but the silence felt different this time. Less rigid, more alive. "Let's all go around the group and explain what we feel confident in." The wind eased for a moment, almost as if listening. Lesly was the first to speak. "Telekinesis," she said simply as she showed her ID. "I can move matter, energy, objects, even elements." Shon gave a small nod. "Teleportation. It's fast, but unpredictable when my mind's scattered. LB said focus isn't just direction, it's permission." Sensi turned her hand toward the dim light reflecting off the dunes. "Light refraction. I can bend and redirect it." Haisley smirked faintly, lightning crackling in shifting colors across her fingertips. "Multicolored lightning. When I think about it, it always seems to be there. Each color feels a bit different, but I usually see turquoise." She looked toward the Bull Pin girls. "Your turn."

Anika held up the coin. "Science. Weather systems, climate balance. I can read patterns." Penn spoke next, her tone calm, analytical, but warm. "Economics. My focus is research and statistics. I studied predicting." London's voice was quiet but assured. "Engineering. Systems, repair, and internal mapping. I can read machinery like language. I may not control energy directly, but I understand how it flows." Imon nodded. "Social systems," she said plainly. "Patterns between people, speech, motives. I read structures." Isabella smiled faintly. "Communication and empathy. I can calm or redirect a crowd faster than most can start one. Words shape energy too. They just move slower sometimes." Kacey adjusted the small panel on her arm, the soft glow pulsing. "Technology and problem solving. I design solutions faster than most people can describe them. My brain's wired for construction, but lately..." she paused, glancing toward Sensi, "I think I'm learning that intuition is also part of invention." Tony adjusted outfit, her eyes scanning the sand. "Science. I like to pay attention to small details." Dot went last. She had been standing a little apart, quiet as always. When she finally spoke, her voice was even and deliberate. "Math," she said. Crly's engraved name shimmered in the light. "It's a strong lineup," he said. "Bear Pin?" The group was curious.

Marcus straightened up to go first. "Social studies. I read patterns, intention and behavior." Ivan leaned in. "Engineering. Specifically, structural mapping. My confidence comes from prediction. I can calculate routes before anyone moves." Hue smiled faintly, the kind that carried ease rather than pride. "Research, but I want to go into neuroscience," he said. Oksao adjusted the sensor on his suit. "Tech operations. I'd say mainly data translation. I'm typically operating in between hardware and instinct." Frederick stepped forward next, his voice measured and composed. "Mathematics. I mainly focus on foresight, probability, rational risk, and data ethics." The circle fell quiet. The alien jet still shimmered faintly in the distance, watching but unmoving. Above them, streaks of violet light wound through the clouds like veins of thought. Crly's mechanical stance softened. Anika looked around at each face, her hand closing gently around the coin. "So there we have it," said Crly, his obvious deflection suggested that he was not going to take his turn to explain himself. The group nodded. In the stillness between breaths, the weather in desert seemed to hum back through the sand which took their attention, subtle but obvious.

"We should get going," Shon said, her voice firm but low. No one argued. The words drifted into the air and stayed there, suspended between. For a moment, no one moved. Marcus glanced at the coin in Anika's hand, then looked toward the horizon, scanning the faint mountains that separated the east from the flats. "If we're covering ground," he started carefully, "it makes sense to split into smaller groups." Sensi nodded, eyes narrowing slightly. "Smaller groups are faster." It was logical and obvious. The kind of reasoning that sounded like survival, not collaboration. Lesly caught on first. "So... by team?" she asked, though her tone made it clear she already knew the answer. Marcus hesitated. "By training," he corrected gently. A quiet ripple of understanding moved through the group. No one said it, but everyone felt it. They'd been shaped by their worlds and molded by different systems, lessons, and expectations. Their huddle seemed to remind them that they had a life beyond the strangers they just met. The Smiley girls, Lesly, Shon, Sensi, and Haisley, instinctively stood together, their stances fluid, adaptive, already reading the air as if it spoke their language. The Bull Pin girls gathered near Anika, their posture deliberate, calculated. Logic in their eyes, method in every breath. They knew their strengths lay in understanding, building, and analyzing to the point of efficiency. A backbone of Civilization 1's legacy. The Bear Pin boys lingered closest to the mountains. They didn't have to speak to fall into formation because discipline was muscle memory. The alien jets flickered again in the distance, its silhouettes unmoving but unmistakably observant, as if witnessing the moment each civilization unconsciously reclaimed its shape. The wind picked up, stirring thin arcs of pink sand that wound between their feet. The group watched wind move the particles of the desert in a single direction, landing at the feet of the Bull Pin girls. Marcus looked at Penn.

He hadn't meant to, but his eyes found her in the space between movement and silence. She stood beside Anika, her focus somewhere distant in a steady calm. But to him, she looked exactly as she had the day they met in the hospital. Tired, unguarded, and human. He remembered the way she had spoken to him, not as a subject or a trainee, but as if she already understood the weight he carried. He'd fallen for her then, quietly and without warning, somewhere between the beep of monitors and the chaos of the unknown outside. Now, he was still waiting for a moment that never seemed to come. He thought about walking toward her, maybe offering to join her team, maybe just asking something simple, like how she was holding up or if she'd slept. But he couldn't figure out what to say. They were dividing by training, by instinct, by everything that made sense in their structured worlds. Every reason to move toward her came with a thousand excuses not to. Penn must have felt it. His hesitation and his stare, because she looked up. Just briefly. Her expression shifted, caught somewhere between surprise and something softer. The air seemed to still between them, just long enough for it to mean something neither of them could name. Then she looked away. Marcus dropped his gaze too, pretending to check his shoes. He wanted to believe this wasn't the end, that the groups weren't splitting for good. No one said it out loud. But the silence between them said otherwise. It had that kind of finality that felt like the end of a chapter rather than the start of one.

Archie sprung above the parting teams, orbiting once before settling between them, his wings catching the violet sky like glass. For a moment, his low hum connected both groups, a reminder that even in separation, they were still being watched over. The wind curled through the group again, carrying the silence between the split groups. Sensi adjusted her ID. "Alright," she said. "Let's move. Let's split up to cover as much ground as possible." Without another word, the groups began to move, soft footfalls fading against the endless pink dunes. Above them, the violet streaks in the sky pulsed once, as though the planet itself acknowledged their silent decision.

9

Antiderivative in Civilization 3

By sunrise, Archie had circled back toward the crowd. His blue and purple glittery frame drifted alongside the horizon of the mountain, his movements steady and deliberate. Every gust of wind translated into data, and every shimmer of violet light in the clouds fed his internal map of Civilization 3's terrain. He hovered for a moment, watching as the two groups began to move into the desert. He tracked their faint bootsteps in the sand. The wind sculpted new hills as quickly as it erased their footprints. Behind them, the alien jet remained still, its lights dimming, then flaring once more, as if acknowledging the hunt had begun. Somewhere between the mountains and the flats, Marcus and Ivan found their first coin. Marcus crouched, brushing away the top layer of sand with the back of his glove. The faint glimmer caught the light and a pink disc the size of a compass lid. Ivan scanned the area with his route-mapper, the handheld device flickering with geometric readouts as it traced the coin's embedded energy signature. "Signal reads stable," he said. "This one's pure." Marcus turned it over in his hand, the etched surface reflecting the violet clouds above. "Then that means it's real," he said quietly, sliding it into a collection vial. Behind them, Frederick marked the coordinates, recording the moment as part of his growing map.

A few miles away, Lesly skimmed the surface with careful eyes, lifting only what moved wrong against the grain. She didn't have much luck, but she enjoyed the way the sand felt against her gloves. Haisley flicked a low, harmless charge to make any near-surface coins give her feedback. She took small steps and repeated the process almost mindlessly as they continued to walk. Sensi bent the glare off the sand so the sparkle stood out like stars. In minutes, they had a pouch that clinked softly. Fourteen coins made a soft clink in their pouch, then fifteen. Shon waved the girls to come close as they agreed to head back to LB. She touched her badge to her shoulder and recalled the local grid. "LB's doorway," she said. The dim lights welcomed them with flickering energy. They released a gentle knock, and the holographic woman opened the door, coffee kettle on the counter. "We've brought you fifteen pink coins," Lesly said. "You found them," LB said. "We found enough to cook and then some," Lesly answered, loosening the pouch into LB's waiting hands. LB's stove woke with a clean, satisfying chime. "Let's place it in the stove," she said, already moving, hands solid with hand-cleaning napkins. She grabbed the pouch full of coins and placed her hand inside its top, grabbing two. "One can power the house for the rest of the month," she said. "Thank you so much!" The girls took a seat around the table as she set the pink coin inside a circular tool that enriched the sides with grain. The machine, which she called a stove, began to slowly heat up as she prepared the food close by. "Do you like coin pizza?" The girls looked at each other and giggled. "You mean brick pizza?" Sensi said. "Oh! Yes, is that what you call it these days? I only have a few ingredients, but we will make the most of what we have," she said. The girls began to talk about their experience in the Pink Desert, amazed at its ecosystem. LB listened attentively, eager to answer any questions that would be typical of a newcomer.

A few minutes later, the front door slid open again. Three girls stepped in, dressed in matching grey sweatpants and sweatshirts. Their clothes were worn, but their eyes were alert. One girl, Jessica, had blonde hair pulled into two straight high ponytails. Beside her was Atom, her jet-black hair styled the same way. The smallest, Eon, wore her hair in tight little buns. They're demeanor was worn, clearly tired from being in the sun all day. They seemed to be out of breath, as if they were just training. "LB!" they called out, voices overlapping in relief. They froze as soon as they saw the newcomers, Shon, Lesly, Haisley, and Sensi gathered in the kitchen. "We... saw people in the desert," one of them said cautiously, eyes darting between the four. "Who are they?" said Atom? LB smiled softly. "Guests," she said. "Come in, everyone. This is Shon, Lesly, Haisley, and Sensi. And these are my girls, Jessica, Atom, and Eon." The air shifted as introductions passed around the room. The grey-clad trio hesitated, exchanging glances, then offered shy smiles. "They train here," LB explained, placing a gentle hand on Jessica's shoulder. "They're from a place called Factory Galaxy," she said. "Factory Galaxy?" Lesly echoed. LB nodded. "It's a location that focuses on creation, machines, materials, replication. But not ability. These three are orphans. No one there was teaching them how to understand what they are, so I've been guiding them quietly." Jessica spoke up first, voice thin but sure. "LB's been showing us how to control our energy patterns." Atom added, "In Factory Galaxy, everything's built. No one ever asks why it should be built." Sensi smiled faintly. "If this isn't Factory Galaxy, what do you call this place?" said Shon. LB set a tray of small round crusts onto the counter, her tone shifting toward something more serious. "You're standing in what we call the Antiderivative." "The what?" Haisley asked, leaning forward. "The Antiderivative," LB repeated. "We're a group of people who started as a research hub a few decades back. We have slowly transgressed into a race that eliminates illness. Everything bad gets zeroed out, like in an equation. The equation we use is designed to accelerate the creation of healthy cells at a rate faster than the body's decaying ones." Eon leaned closer, eyes wide, hearing this for the first time. "So, the bad cells get... zeroed out?" "Exactly." LB said. "For every cell that breaks down, two healthy ones take its place. When that balance shifts, the decaying cells lose ground from multiplying. They get outnumbered and overwritten. Its system recalibrates and returns the body to health." The room went quiet, the only sound was the soft hum of the pink-coin stove.

"That's... incredible," Shon said. "It's the foundation of this city," LB said. "The Antiderivative is a discovery that keeps everything alive, people, plants, even the sand. The desert itself is part of the healing system, now that we use the pink coins to support us." Lesly blinked, realization dawning. "Then the pink coins..." LB observed. "Are fragments of that process. They store the same regenerative energy that sustains this land." The girls exchanged looks. Sensi stood. "Our friends are still out there...Anika, Marcus, the others. If the desert's part of this system, maybe they're messing things up?" said Lesly. LB's gaze turned toward the window, where the horizon shimmered under a growing storm. "It doesn't work like this. But, a storm is brewing, you should go," she said softly. "The desert remembers its own." The Smiley girls stood up from the table, energized. They thanked LB, waved to Jessica, Atom, and Eon, and stepped once more into the shifting pink sands. Archie fluttered above them, wings glinting in the light, guiding them toward the storm and the friends still searching beneath it.

10

Bull Pin University Arrives

The horizon flickered as the Smiley girls returned to the pink sands, their boots landing causing a small ripple. The air was dense with the electric hush that came before a storm. Now that they knew about The Antiderivative, Lesly began to think that maybe someone was controlling the weather and causing storms on purpose. "Maybe it's a sign to leave?" said Lesly. "You could be right," said Shon, sort of concerned. The alien jets were still there, it anchored beside the Bear Pin and two Bull Pin jets. Through the tinted glass, the aliens could be seen talking quietly, hands curled around warm cups of coffee. Their laughter was calm, casual even. Meanwhile, near the close mountains, Anika, Penn, London, Crly, and the rest of the Bull Pin group were approaching. Their collection packs jingled faintly, proof of success. The coins they'd found glowed with a subdued pulse, but their faces were tense. Crly's sensors flickered rapidly as he adjusted the frequency on his tracking device. The signal kept cutting in and out. He frowned. "It's picking up a familiar signal, but I can't translate the details." Kacey and Tony tried to help him out. "Could it be interference from the alien ship?" "No," Crly said quietly. "Something further away."

He tracked the satellite scanner and tracked its movements towards the edge of the galaxy. His visual processors magnified the image. Five metallic figures were moving fast across the galaxy field and one of them was unmistakably Grgy. He was accompanied by four other robotic associates. Crly's circuits pulsed in response. "It's Grgy. He's coming," said Crly. Anika's breath caught. "Here?" she said. Crly nodded. "Straight for us." The group exchanged quick glances. The calm that had defined the day began to fracture.

They moved quickly to the newer Bull Pin University ship, sleeker and more advanced than the one Anika, London, and Penn had arrived in. Sensi, Lesly Shon and Haisley see them run to the jet from a distance. The inside hummed with power. The walls glowed faintly, reacting to the crew's presence as if aware of their unease. "What's the plan? Teamwork is key right now." London asked, her voice steady but low. "What should we do?" Penn asked. "The guys are still out there. If Grgy's coming, heading back to Bull Pin doesn't make sense." Anika's fingers drummed lightly against the console. "If we leave now, we risk losing them. But if we stay..." She trailed off.

Haisley and Lesly knocked on the jet door. Isabella opened the hatch, and looked at them with a concern, "We have a problem. Something's heading this way." The girls piled in, making the jet a tight place to get comfortable. The causality of the situation shifted the tone in the room. "How bad?" said Shon. "Grgy-level bad," Penn replied. A silence filled the room before Sensi answered, "What do you think they want?" asked Sensi. The Smiley girls spoke softly among themselves, their voices blending between English and Spanish. "¿Qué hacemos ahora?" Lesly asked, her eyes darting to the sky. "No sabemos cómo regresar," Sensi said, frustration lacing her tone. "¿Y si Shon intenta teletransportarse?" Haisley offered. Shon hesitated. "No estoy segura que funcione así..." she said. They turned to look at her. "Even if I could," Shon said, switching back to English, "I don't know where we'd land. The storm's making it harder to focus. And I don't have a map of our island." "So, we wait?" Lesly asked. Sensi bit her lip. "If we go to the aliens, we don't know what to expect. If we stay here, we're sitting targets," she said. For a moment, no one spoke. The ship's systems hummed softly, like a heartbeat. Then Anika exhaled, her mind returning to the only place that had ever felt remotely stable lately. "2012," she said quietly. "Civilization 0." The others looked at her. "We've been there before," she continued. London nodded slowly. "We could wait for Marcus and the others. Tell them the plan. Then leave." Penn crossed her arms. "You think they'll make it in time?" said Isabella. "They should," Penn said firmly. "They seem to always do." said Penn. Outside, the wind began to rise, scattering pink dust across the dunes. The alien ship's engines hummed low, as if bracing. In the distance, five bright jets broke through the upper atmosphere...it was Grgy's fleet.

Crly looked out through the jet's viewport, their sensors glowing faint blue. "He's here." The first jet descended like a comet, landing hard enough to shake the ground. The others followed, forming a tight formation that shimmered against the storm-lit sky. Shocked by their innovation cycle, Crly noticed that their jet speed was 10x faster than the machines he was familiar with. No one moved. It was clear that cultural relativism wasn't a bargaining chip. The Smiley girls stood near the hatch, ready to teleport if they had to. The aliens dimmed their lights and powered down visible systems, their chatter fading to whispers. For a long, suspended moment, no one breathed. Then the comm crackled to life, Crly's voice steady and low. "Everyone... hold position. If this goes wrong, get to the Smiley team. They know the way out." Sensi looked at Lesly, then at Shon. The storm's glow reflected in their visors. "What about LB?" Shon said softly. "If it comes to it... we should go back to the Antiderivative." Outside, lightning fractured across the pink desert sky. Haisley's hands released a gentle multicolored push of electricity. The five approaching jets cast long shadows over the sand as the alien ships pulsed with internal light. The desert gasped like a drawn breath, exhaling their new social construct, waiting to see what would happen next. And somewhere above them, Archie circled the storm's edge, embracing everything as the Pink Planet welcomed more visitors from Bull Pin University.

Reading Comprehension Appendix

The STREAMSS Framework builds upon the traditional STEAM model and expands the scope of education to include Science, Technology, Reading-to-Research, Engineering, Arts, Mathematics, and Social Studies/Social Justice, redefining how we understand literacy and learning. It strengthens STEAM by emphasizing three crucial dimensions, Reading, Research, and Social Studies, to ensure that comprehension, inquiry, and civic awareness remain central to interdisciplinary education. Both Reading and Research are foundational to the development of critical inquiry, comprehension, and communication, skills that are increasingly essential in modern education.

In the STREAMSS Framework, the "R" is interchangeable and depends on the learner's educational stage. The framework operates on a two-tier system: in primary education, "R" represents *Reading*, emphasizing comprehension and literacy development. In secondary education, it transitions to *Research*, focusing on inquiry, analysis, and synthesis. This structure ensures that STREAMSS adapts to the learner's cognitive growth, guiding them from foundational understanding to independent exploration.

As discussed in *Project Board Game's* analysis of STREAMSS, early literacy is not simply a support skill but a discipline that enables every other form of learning (Project Board Game, 2024). Reading builds decoding ability, fluency, and comprehension, each serving as the intellectual infrastructure for understanding complex ideas across the disciplines. When students fail to achieve reading proficiency by the third or fourth grade, research consistently shows that their ability to access content across disciplines declines. Reading, therefore, must be explicitly named and taught as a discipline, not merely embedded as a secondary focus of language arts.

In the upper grades, "R" evolves into Research, signaling a shift from reading comprehension to inquiry-based exploration. The STEAMS Initiative article "Reimagining STEAMS to Include "R" for Research" emphasizes that research literacy is essential for navigating today's information-rich environment (STEAMS Initiative, 2024). Students must learn not just to absorb facts, but to question them, and to collect data, evaluate credibility, and synthesize perspectives across disciplines. In this way, Research in STREAMSS represents the active application of comprehension, moving from understanding to investigation.

Comprehension and research are inseparable. Reading comprehension builds the cognitive scaffolding that enables students to recognize relationships between concepts, and research extends that comprehension into new discoveries. The connection between the two support the STREAMSS pedagogy. Both functions require vocabulary mastery, and an awareness of how words change in meaning across discipline. This is where the Vocabulary Appendix becomes essential. It transforms reading from passive recognition into interdisciplinary understanding. Each word in the list was selected to help readers interpret language not only within the literary context of *Journey into the Pink Desert, Love Across Time*, but across the STREAMSS disciplines.

In practical terms, this approach prepares students for academic success and practical comprehension. STREAMSS encourages comprehension as an entry point into global awareness and research as the means of constructing solutions. By practicing reading as inquiry, students become more adept at evaluating evidence, understanding bias, and applying critical reasoning. These skills are central to both academic and professional environments. STREAMSS also reflects a moral dimension. By incorporating Social Studies (or Social Justice), the model insists that comprehension and research must serve a greater purpose, which is understanding humanity and advancing equity. Reading becomes an act of empathy, allowing students to see through different perspectives. Research becomes a tool of agency, enabling them to address real-world issues through evidence-based reasoning. They shape informed citizens capable of ethical decision-making and innovative problem-solving.

In the broader educational landscape, STREAMSS bridges the divide between the sciences and the humanities. It asserts that comprehension (the ability to read deeply, interpret context, and recognize nuance) is a universal skill that underpins all disciplines. Likewise, research, is what transforms learning from memorization into understanding. The vocabulary list within this appendix is a guide for how readers can approach texts, questions, and ideas across disciplines with intellectual flexibility.

By integrating Reading and Research as equal pillars alongside Science, Technology, Engineering, Arts, Mathematics, and Social Studies, STREAMSS acknowledges that knowledge is interconnected. Every discipline depends on comprehension for access and on research for advancement. Vocabulary becomes the medium through which these processes unfold and each term is an opportunity to expand understanding, challenge assumptions, and connect insights across fields. Ultimately, STREAMSS is a philosophy of learning that situates literacy at the heart of discovery and understanding.

Vocabulary List A: Foundations Level

1. **Innovation** (T, E) - A new idea or improvement to an existing method.
2. **Ethical** (SS, R) - Guided by what is morally right.
3. **Sufficiency** (E, M) - Being adequate or enough to meet needs.
4. **Humanity** (SS) - Compassion and kindness toward others.

5. **Survival** (S, SS) - Continuing to live or function through difficulty.
6. **Faith** (SS) - Trust or belief in something greater than oneself.
7. **Discipline** (M, E, R) - Consistent practice or obedience to rules.
8. **Journey** (SS) - A process of growth and discovery.
9. **Courage** (SS) - The ability to act bravely in the face of fear.
10. **Purpose** (R, SS, A) - A reason or intention that gives meaning to actions.
11. **Respect** (SS) - Regard or consideration for others.
12. **Curiosity** (S, R) - The desire to learn or understand something new.
13. **Harmony** (SS) - A balanced or peaceful relationship among people or things.
14. **Kindness** (SS) - The quality of being friendly and caring.
15. **Promise** (SS) - A commitment or declaration to act.
16. **Hope** (SS) - Expectation of positive outcomes or change.
17. **Teamwork** (SS, E) - Cooperative effort to achieve a shared goal.
18. **Growth** (M, S) - Development through learning and experience.
19. **Character** (A) - The moral and ethical qualities of a person.
20. **Imagination** (A, E, T, R, S) - The ability to form new ideas or concepts.
21. **Responsibility** (SS) - Being accountable for actions or duties.
22. **Perseverance** (E, T, R) - Continued effort despite challenges.
23. **Friendship** (SS) - A bond based on trust and mutual care.
24. **Empathy** (S, R, SS) - Understanding and sharing another's feelings.
25. **Adaptation** (S, E, T) - Adjusting to new situations or environments.
26. **Observation** (S, R) - Paying close attention to detail.
27. **Integrity** (SS) - Doing the right thing even when no one is watching.
28. **Discovery** (R, S, T) - Finding or learning something new.
29. **Balance** (M, S,) - A state of stability or fairness.
30. **Choice** (SS, M) - The act of making a decision.

31. **Belonging** (SS) - Feeling accepted within a group or community.

Vocabulary List B: Applied Level

36. **Civilization** (SS) - A developed human society with structured systems.
37. **Algorithmic** (T, M) - Controlled by step-by-step logical procedures.
38. **Autonomy** (SS, R) - Independence in thought or action.
39. **Evolution** (S, R, SS) - Gradual change or development over time.
40. **Compassion** (SS) - Deep concern for others' suffering.
41. **Ethos** (SS) - The guiding beliefs of a community or system.
42. **Innovation Cycle** (T, R) - The process through which new ideas are developed and refined.
43. **System** (E, S) - An organized set of parts working together.
44. **Network** (T, E) - A connected structure for communication or exchange.
45. **Advocacy** (SS) - Public support for a cause or idea.
46. **Coexist** (S, SS) - Living peacefully with differences.
47. **Innovation Gap** (M, E, T) - The difference between those with access to technology and those without.
48. **Perception** (T, A, R) - How something is understood or interpreted.
49. **Reflection** (R) - Thoughtful consideration or review.
50. **Collaboration** (E, T, R, A) - Working together on a shared project.
51. **Reform** (SS) - Improvement or change to make a system better.
52. **Symbolism** (A) - Use of images or objects to represent ideas.
53. **Conflict** (SS) - A struggle between opposing forces or ideas.
54. **Perspective** (A) - A particular viewpoint or way of understanding.
55. **Interdependence** (SS, S, E) - Mutual reliance between people or systems.

56. **Equilibrium** (S, M, R) - A balanced state between forces or influences.

Vocabulary List C: Bridge Level

66. **Transcendence** (RM, SS) - Rising above limits or ordinary experiences.
67. **Epistemology** (R)- The study of knowledge and its validity.
68. **Cognitive Dissonance** (R, S) - Conflict between beliefs and behavior.
69. **Post-humanism** (T, A) - The idea that technology reshapes human identity.
70. **Moral Agency** (S) - The ability to make ethical choices independently.
71. **Systemic Reform** (SS, M) - Structural change that affects entire institutions.
72. **Metacognition** (S, R) - Awareness of one's own thinking process.
73. **Empirical** (S, R) - Based on observation or experience.
74. **Paradigm** (R) - A model or framework that defines understanding.
75. **Ethnography** (R) - Research focused on observing social behavior and culture.
76. **Symbolic Interaction** (SS) - Meaning created through human interaction.
77. **Phenomenon** (S) - An observable event or occurrence.
78. **Automation** (T, E) - The use of technology to operate without human input.
79. **Sustainability** (S, E) - Maintaining balance to preserve future resources.
80. **Ethnobotany** (S, R) - Study of how people use plants in culture or medicine.
81. **Neuroscience** (S, T) - The scientific study of the brain and nervous system.

82. **Data Ethics** (R, T, M) - Moral principles in collecting and using information.
83. **Ecological Footprint** (S, SS) - The impact of human activity on the environment.
84. **Globalization** (SS) - The process of worldwide connection and exchange.
85. **Cultural Relativism** (SS) - Understanding cultures based on their own context.
86. **Digital Citizenship** (E, T, SS) - Responsible participation in online environments.
87. **Cybernetics** (T, E, M) - Study of systems, feedback, and control in machines and living things.
88. **Pluralism** (SS) - Acceptance of multiple perspectives and beliefs.
89. **Causality** (M, S) - The relationship between cause and effect.
90. **Heuristics** (R, S) - Mental shortcuts used for problem-solving.
91. **Social Construct** (SS) - An idea shaped by collective belief rather than fact.

References

Reference List (APA 7th Edition):

Project Board Game. (2024, July 15). *An analysis on STREAMSS for K–6 and 7–12, and the case for reading or research as a discipline.* Project Board Game.

STEAMS Initiative. (2024, April 22). *Reimagining STEAMS to include "R" for research: Creating STREAMSS.* STEAMS Initiative.

Character Sheet

Anika (Environmental Science)

Anika's calm presence mirrors the serenity of the desert itself; quiet, patient, and deeply attuned to her surroundings. She studies the natural world as both a scientist and a believer, tracing how each grain of sand, gust of wind, and droplet of water reflects order. Guided by observation, she finds meaning in the unseen systems that sustain life. To the group, Anika is grounding; a reminder that renewal begins awareness meets.

Penn (Research)

Penn is logic embodied; steady, deliberate, and intuitive. She views every challenge as a tradeoff of risk and reward, always weighing the unseen costs of every choice. Though analytical, her mind carries warmth; she sees the relations in numbers and the emotion behind every decision. Penn's curiosity about systems of value drives her to understand not only currency and trade but the moral economies that shape relationships. Beneath her precision lies quiet empathy, a soft understanding that order without compassion breeds imbalance.

London (Engineering)

London's strength lies in her endurance; a quiet resilience that refuses to fade. Where others see broken machinery, she sees blueprints waiting to be reimagined. Her designs are metaphors for perseverance, bridges between limitation and possibility. She transforms pain into purpose, showing that innovation is born not from perfection but persistence. London's presence teaches the group that engineering is more than mechanics; it's the art of rebuilding, both systems and mindset, when the world breaks down.

Imon (Social Justice)

Bold and unyielding, Imon speaks truth to imbalance. Her words strike with precision, challenging structures built on silence. She has a gift for transforming frustration into advocacy. Every debate, every stand, every question she poses shakes the foundation of complacency. Imon believes justice isn't granted; it's built, piece by piece, through courage and grace. She reminds others that morality isn't passive but participatory, that real change begins when someone refuses to look away. To her, leadership is not about authority; it's about amplifying voices unheard.

Isabella (Arts Communication)

Isabella communicates where words falter. Through her communication, she channels empathy into motion, colors, tones, and phrases that bridge hearts when logic fails. Her calm presence makes her the group's emotional interpreter, translating conflict into connection. She sees art not as performance but as service; a universal language that restores amid struggle. Her creative intuition allows her to perceive emotion as rhythm, each expression a note in the collective song of their journey.

Kacey (Technology)

Sharp-minded and forward-thinking, Kacey thrives where curiosity meets challenge. She sees technology as a living extension of thought; an evolving dialogue between human creativity and machine precision. Her innovations often blur the line between logic and art, producing tools that reflect empathy as much as efficiency. Fearless in experimentation, she isn't driven by invention for its own sake but by how it can uplift communities. Beneath her confident exterior is a restless visionary who believes that every code written should have a conscience.

Tony (Science)

Tony's curiosity drives her ambition. She approaches every unknown as a puzzle, driven by the belief that understanding science imperative. Her notebooks are filled with sketches and data, all written in special detail. Tony's methodical nature balances her innate sense of wonder, allowing her to find patterns in chaos and hope in experimentation. She's fascinated not only by how things work but why they exist, seeking the story behind every structure.

Dot (Mathematics)

Dot processes the unseen, mapping meaning in what others overlook. She reads the world in equations, symmetry, and sequence; every variable a story waiting to be solved. Her mathematical intuition allows her to detect rhythm in randomness, bridging logic with emotion. She brings mathematical insight that often steers the group in moments of confusion. For Dot, numbers are not cold or distant, but can be used as tool for love.

Marcus (Social Studies)

Marcus is a leader forged in discipline but defined by reflection. He once studied the difference between authority and control. His experience taught him that guidance grows from empathy. He values the study of leadership style blended with strategy with compassion, a rare balance that earns trust rather than demands it. Marcus views every challenge as a collaborative mission, measuring success by unity rather than dominance. His discipline teaches him that decisions come not from impulse but introspection, rooted in the idea that great leaders listen twice before they speak once.

Frederick (Mathematics)

Frederick is a philosopher at heart and he drifts between data and dreams, piecing together patterns that others dismiss as coincidence. He studies math theories that often stretch beyond practicality, yet they reveal ideas that anchor math into practical equations. He's fascinated by connections, how logic and reality coexist, how reason and intuition merge. While some see abstraction, Frederick sees possibility. His meticulous research and relentless curiosity drive the group toward understanding the bigger picture, proving that every theory, no matter how obscure, begins with the courage to question.

Ivan (Engineering)

Ivan's presence is steady and reassuring, the silent craftsman of both machines and morale. His understanding of design extends beyond form and function; he builds with intention, ensuring that what he creates sustains both structure and spirit. Reliable and grounded, Ivan often takes on the role of quiet problem-solver, the one who keeps systems and people running smoothly. His empathy shows in the details, from the stability of a bridge to the safety of a companion.

Hue (Reading)

Hue listens before he speaks, reading tone as fluently as language. His gift for reading makes him a natural diplomat, capable of dissolving tension through conversation and understanding. He sees dialogue as architecture, something to be built carefully, brick by brick, with patience and grace. When conflict arises, Hue mediates with wisdom, choosing clarity over competition. His humor and warmth disarm even the most guarded individuals, reminding everyone that communication isn't about winning, it's about connection.

Oksao (Technology)

Oksao is deliberate, technical, and introspective; a master of systems who operates like the quiet hum of a machine running perfectly in sync. He sees digital patterns as languages of intention, each algorithm carrying emotion and rhythm. His analytical mind is unmatched, but it's his discipline that sets him apart. Oksao works not just to optimize performance, but to ensure machine functionality.

Courtesy (Sound Manipulation)

Clad in her bright orange uniform, Courtesy commands attention the moment she enters a room. Her gift, Sound Manipulation, allows her to bend air into rhythm, shaping invisible sound waves as if they were glass. She can amplify whispers into thunder, turn silence into pressure, and mold frequencies across air, water, or solid ground. Her strength isn't control, it's knowing when to hold back. Confident and magnetic, she moves with rhythm itself, a reminder that sound carries both creation and destruction.

Yola (Echolocation)

Measured and analytical, Yola sees the world through vibration and reflection. Her power, Echolocation, grants her sight beyond sight, a mental blueprint of everything around her through returning sound waves. No illusion or shadow can hide from her. Calm under pressure, Yola interprets the world as music made visible, a constant conversation between motion and truth.

Haven (Singing Mastery)

Radiant and composed, Haven's voice carries the strength of serenity. With her power, Singing Mastery, she possesses perfect pitch, infinite range, and complete emotional command. When she sings, the air thickens with harmony; light bends to her rhythm. Haven's tone is both elegance and calm, the embodiment of balance between art and influence.

Lesly (Telekinesis)

Lesly possesses the power of Telekinesis, the ability to move and control objects using only her mind. Telekinesis forms the foundation for many advanced powers centered around control and manipulation. With training, Lesly could reach incredible precision, manipulating matter and energy at their smallest levels. In its most advanced form, telekinesis can extend to influencing elements of space and time. Lesly's natural curiosity and self-discipline make her a steady force, symbolizing both mental strength and the responsibility that comes with great power.

Sensi (Chromakinesis)

Sensi's ability is Skin Manipulation, allowing her to alter her appearance by blending seamlessly into her surroundings or taking on any texture, color, or density. Her power extends beyond camouflage, she can manipulate the properties of skin itself, both her own and others', adjusting smoothness, sensitivity, and resilience. Her adaptability and awareness give her an edge in any situation, reflecting her balance of confidence and control.

Shon (Teleportation)

Shon can Teleport, moving instantaneously from one location to another without crossing the space between. Her power allows her to transfer herself or others through various mechanisms, from warping water and bending light to rearrangement at the precise level. She embodies freedom, agility, and exploration, representing the courage to move forward and the wisdom to navigate between worlds.

Haisley (Energy)

Haisley's ability is Energy, the capacity to generate and control lightning across a spectrum of colors, each color carrying distinct properties. She can summon multiple bolts of varying hues or channel a single multi-colored surge of immense power. This skill represents a form of electricity manipulation, fusing strength with beauty. Haisley's innovative spirit and scientific curiosity makes her the "storm mind" of her team, constantly exploring the balance between volatility and illumination.

About the Author

Grlpire is more than a reading program, it's a creative education platform that transforms literature into an interactive learning experience. Rooted in the STREAMSS framework (Science, Technology, Reading/Research, Engineering, Arts, Mathematics, and Social Studies/Social Justice), Grlpire connects stories to real-world learning through books, curriculum, workshops, and hands-on activities inspired by its original content universe.

At the heart of Grlpire is *Journey Into the Pink Desert*, a storyworld that blends exploration, resilience, and character-driven discovery. Its landscapes, pastel pink, purple, green and brown sands, towering rock formations, cacti, and winding turquoise waters, give readers more than a setting. They offer a pathway into interdisciplinary thinking. Every chapter, character, and journey becomes an opportunity to explore big ideas: the science of ecosystems, the technology of survival, the research to understand c the engineering behind movement and structures, the art woven into a new civilization, the math hidden in patterns and problem-solving, and the social studies themes that shape community, culture, and choice.

Grlpire's approach is simple: reading should spark curiosity, not feel like another task. By blending storytelling with interdisciplinary exploration, learners discover that reading isn't just about turning pages, it's about developing understanding, building connections, and learning one idea at a time. Through STREAMSS-aligned curriculum tools, inquiry-based challenges, character-themed activities, and immersive resources, Grlpire helps readers engage deeply with both the story and the world around them.

Whether someone is diving into the Pink Desert for adventure, joining a STREAMSS workshop, or exploring one of our educational tools, Grlpire encourages every learner to approach reading with confidence, imagination, and purpose. Discover the universe. Explore the ideas. Grow with the journey.

Learn more about Grlpire today at www.grlpire.com.